UNCOMMON WEATHER

ALASKA LITERARY SERIES

Peggy Shumaker, Series Editor

ALASKA
LITERARY
SERIES

The Alaska Literary Series publishes poetry, fiction, and literary nonfiction. Successful manuscripts have a strong connection to Alaska or the circumpolar north, are written by people living in the far north, or both. We prefer writing that makes the northern experience available to the world, and we choose manuscripts that offer compelling literary insights into the human condition.

Armor and Ornament
by Christopher Lee Miles

Be-Hooved by Mar Ka

Benchmarks by Richard Dauenhauer

Cabin, Clearing, Forest by Zach Falcon

Cabin 135 by Katie Eberhart

The City Beneath the Snow
by Marjorie Kowalski Cole

Cold Latitudes by Rosemary McGuire

Cold Spell by Deb Vanasse

The Cormorant Hunter's Wife
by Joan Kane

*The Creatures at the Absolute Bottom
of the Sea* by Rosemary McGuire

Ends of the Earth by Kate Partridge

Gaining Daylight by Sara Loewen

*Gagaan X̱'usyee / Below the Foot of the
Sun* by X̱'unei Lance Twitchell

The Geography of Water
by Mary Emerick

Human Being Songs by Jean Anderson

I Follow in the Dust She Raises
by Linda Martin

In the Quiet Season and Other Stories
by Martha Amore

Just Between Us by David McElroy

A Ladder of Cranes by Tom Sexton

Leavetakings by Corinna Cook

Li Bai Rides a Celestial Dolphin Home
by Tom Sexton

Of Darkness and Light by Wendy Erd

Oil and Water by Mei Mei Evans

Old Woman with Berries in Her Lap
by Vivian Faith Prescott

Overwinter by Jeremy Pataky

The Rabbits Could Sing
by Amber Flora Thomas

River of Light by John Morgan
and Kesler Woodward

Roughly for the North
by Carrie Ayagaduk Ojanen

Sailing by Ravens by Holly J. Hughes

Spirit Things
by Lara Messersmith-Glavin

Threadbare by Mary Kudenov

Trouble will Save You by David Nikki
Crouse

Upriver by Carolyn Kremers

Water Mask by Monica Devine

Water the Rocks Make by David
McElroy

Whiteout by Jessica Goodfellow

Wild Rivers Wild Rose
by Sarah Birdsall

Uncommon Weather

ALASKA STORIES

Richard Chiappone

ALASKA LITERARY SERIES

University of Alaska Press • FAIRBANKS

Published by University of Alaska Press

An imprint of University Press of Colorado
1580 North Logan Street, Suite 660
PMB 39883
Denver, Colorado 80203–1942

Printed in the United States of America

 The University Press of Colorado is a proud member of
Association of University Presses.

The University Press of Colorado is a cooperative publishing enterprise supported, in part, by Adams State University, Colorado State University, Fort Lewis College, Metropolitan State University of Denver, University of Alaska Fairbanks, University of Colorado, University of Denver, University of Northern Colorado, University of Wyoming, Utah State University, and Western Colorado University.

∞ This paper meets the requirements of the ANSI/NISO Z39.48–1992 (Permanence of Paper).

ISBN: 978-1-64642-635-5 (hardcover)
ISBN: 978-1-64642-636-2 (paperback)
ISBN: 978-1-64642-637-9 (ebook)
https://doi.org/10.5876/9781646426379

Library of Congress Cataloging-in-Publication Data

Names: Chiappone, Richard, author.
Title: Uncommon weather : Alaska stories / Richard Chiappone.
Description: Fairbanks : University of Alaska Press, 2024. |
Series: Alaska literary series.
Identifiers: LCCN 2024002456 (print) | LCCN 2024002457 (ebook) |
ISBN 9781646426355 (hardcover) | ISBN 9781646426362 (paperback) |
ISBN 9781646426379 (ebook)
Subjects: LCGFT: Short stories.
Classification: LCC PS3603.H52 U53 2024 (print) | LCC PS3603.H52 (ebook) |
DDC 813/.6—dc23/eng/20240329
LC record available at https://lccn.loc.gov/2024002456
LC ebook record available at https://lccn.loc.gov/2024002457

Cover illustration: "Knight Island Passage," © Asia Freeman.

To all my students.

Contents

Xtratuf *3*

Angels, Jellies, and Squid *16*

So, Kenny the Sheetrocker Sends for His Girl *29*

Little Wing *35*

Necturus Maculosus *44*

Every Son Must Wonder *53*

Help *69*

Time on the Water *80*

Chekhov's Rule *116*

Mammoth *124*

Uncommon Weather *137*

Special *147*

Acknowledgments *159*

UNCOMMON WEATHER

Xtratuf

Phil McDermott is up on his roof examining the iridescent green moss smothering the shingles when his granddaughter Melanie comes home from her mindfulness seminar, upset and howling with uncontrollable laughter that bleeds into crying. Not the response to meditation he'd hoped for.

It's summer in coastal Alaska, maybe 45°, clouds like wet cement, a persistent cool rain seeping through the big spruce trees surrounding the house. Not a day a man his age would choose to spend on a roof. But suddenly a fifteen-year-old girl lives with him, and Phil's taking his responsibilities seriously now.

From up here he can see Kachemak Bay, where a boxy white cruise ship appears in the layered mists like an invading troop transport. With the pandemic feeling more and more in the distant past, projections are that this is going to be a very big year for tourism in Homer. Across the bay, oblivious to economic forecasts and every other concern of men, glaciers chew through the stony mountains as they have for millennia, while Phil is reluctant to buy metal roofing that will outlive him by mere decades.

Melanie pedals up the driveway on her bike wearing her bright yellow Helly Hansen slicker. In spite of the cool rain, she's riding barefoot and laughing out loud, an ominous sign that she's slipping again. By the pitch of her hilarity, Phil has a feeling this could be a bad one.

"Melanie!" he shouts down to her.

Startled, she chokes off her laughter and gapes up into the wet sky like she's just heard God beckoning from somewhere above the spruce tops. Her face, framed by the yellow rubber hood, is festooned with shiny piercings. Several strands of bright blue hair lie plastered to her forehead. Rain mingles with the tears on her cheeks. She finally sees Phil on the roof and gasps. "Pops?" She's sniffles. "What the fuck are you doing on the roof?"

"What happened, honey?"

She steps off the bike and yelps in pain from the sharp gravel under her bare feet. "Someone stole my boots from the meditation room at the wellness center!"

"Okay," he sighs. "I'll be right down."

*   *   *

In the house, they peel off their raingear and she drops into a kitchen chair, quiet now, but eyes still wild as she massages her wet, wrinkled toes. She's ridden home barefoot through the town's pitted and puddled streets to avoid soaking the beautiful wool socks she knitted in rehab. She's also learning to spin yarn, another activity he has encouraged since her arrival a month ago. Despite the generational differences, their relationship has been mostly peaceful most of that time, and he thinks they're going to be all right. Still, he has locked up his guns.

When Melanie was a week old, her father, Phil's son John, committed suicide. Soon after, Melanie's mother Sandy declared Homer unlivable for a young widow: winters too cold, too wet, and too long; summers too cold, too wet, and too short. She took baby Melanie and left for warmer, drier climes. Over the intervening fifteen years, Phil has mailed checks for his granddaughter to every major city in the American Sunbelt. He should've made an effort to see Melanie more often, should've sent for her sooner, and he knows it. But he and his wife Polly split around that dark time too, and he never reached out to Polly again either. So, with no one to blame but himself, he's on his own now with his granddaughter, and he has to remind himself that under that bright blue haystack of hair, the spidery tattoos, those lips so heavily pierced they look like they've been riveted onto her face, lies a wounded teenage girl. He's taken time off from his boatyard to be home with her. She is not to be left alone for long.

He takes a chair across the kitchen table from her. "Mel, do you have this under control, honey?"

"They stole my boots from the wellness center!" she says, and then she's laughing again, the hysteria rising. She shrieks, "The fucking wellness center! That's funny!" But knowing what's funny and what isn't can be a challenge for her.

* * *

Phil once had an Uncle Henry who laughed at all the wrong times. When Henry was a teenager he was diagnosed with what was then called hebephrenic schizophrenia. Henry was in and out of mental institutions for most of his life. More than once Phil overheard his parents discussing the barbaric so-called treatments his uncle endured and he lay awake nights throughout his own adolescence worrying where the disease might next rear its awful head in their family. Phil got lucky. His son didn't fare so well. And now his granddaughter.

Melanie's doctor told Phil not to worry too much about labels. "Just think of it as a possibly temporary imbalance in brain chemistry."

Her fondness for recreational drugs complicates things. Do the drugs make her crazy, or does her craziness incline her to do drugs? In Phil's mind, this is a chicken-or-egg dilemma that simply baffles him.

Under advisement from his girlfriend Ingrid—she's the principal at Homer High School and seems to understand teenagers as well as any adult can—Phil is keeping Melanie involved in wholesome activities until school resumes in the fall. Wholesome activities like mindfulness, knitting, and spinning. He's vaguely aware that in bigger cities "spinning" is something that is done on bicycles that go nowhere, and that it may or may not be related to something else called Pilates. But in this town spinning involves animal hair, skein-winders, and a commitment to sustainability.

This is that kind of place, Phil thinks. Or it used to be.

Now that Melanie has the laughter under control, he thinks they should try to talk calmly about the incident. "Okay, someone stole your boots from the wellness center," he says, hoping that saying it aloud will minimize his astonishment. Homer has just a single two-lane road connecting it to the contiguous highway system of North America, and the town seems to Phil remote from the ugliness of the times. But lately the guys at the boatyard tell him he should lock his truck every time he steps out of it, and his insurance company would like him to unleash ferocious hounds inside the fence at night. He's not buying their dire assessment of local circumstances. Not yet anyway.

"Maybe it was an accident," he says to Melanie. "Who would steal used boots?"

"Druggies," she says, like that's almost too obvious to articulate. She pulls thick wool socks out of a pocket and tugs them onto her chilled feet. "They'd scrape the enamel off your teeth if they could get 5 bucks for it."

The casual certainty with which she declares this is disturbing, yet he's happy to hear her say "druggies" in that vaguely general way the word is thrown around by people his age who have never even seen hard drugs. If only that were true of Melanie. The deal he made with his daughter-in-law was this: he paid for his granddaughter's rehab; he gets to make sure she stays clean now that she's out. Whatever the guys at the yard say, he's pretty sure Homer is still a hell of a lot safer than the many distant cities Melanie and her sun-seeking mother have sampled.

"Druggies?"

Melanie nods. "I'm telling you, Pops, they're taking over your town. Read the paper."

Every Thursday Melanie faithfully reads the *Homer News*, the town's weekly paper. Phil is encouraged by her interest in local life. He's looking for positive signs in *everything* she does. That's not always easy. This week she pointed out an article about the extraordinary number of discarded syringes people have been finding on the beach near the Alaska State Ferry terminal.

Still struggling with the loss of her boots, Melanie sighs. "Those were real Xtratufs. Fuckers cost Mom a fortune."

She had, in fact, gotten off the plane in Anchorage wearing the brown, calf-high rubber footwear and the giant yellow raincoat, looking like she'd just escaped from a Winslow Homer painting. She wore them in the truck on the drive all the way down the Kenai Peninsula to the town. Melanie won't set foot in the twin-engine prop planes the commuter airline uses. Her view is that the big jets are safe enough, but anything with propellers is a death trap with wings.

"I'm sorry about this," he says. "I'm sorry it ruined your meditation today."

Slipping her warmed feet into clunky, blaze-orange garden clogs, Melanie confesses she's not sure mindfulness is right for her. "Too focused. I sort of just got my brain back from the cleaners, you know? I want to let it wander wherever it wants to go right now. Is that okay?"

"Sure, honey." Frankly, he's relieved that this didn't take root. Mindfulness sounds suspiciously like the kind of thing a well-meaning enthusiast might insist her grandfather join her in. He's determined to help her, of course. But if he has to become a better person himself, all bets are off. "Fine. Let's forget mindfulness for now."

She already has. "Didn't they used to, like, hang guys for stealing boots in the Old West days?"

"I think that was horse thieves," he says, picturing a horseless and bootless cowboy facing a long walk across the desert in his stocking feet, a vision that seems not unlike living with a teenage girl at his age.

Melanie frowns. "Horse thieves, horse shit. I thought this place was going to be different."

"It *is* different. Or . . ." His pause is unintentional, but long. ". . . It was, once."

"It was different 'once'?" She snickers. "Oh, Pops, you are *so* old. Is that painful?"

She has no idea.

But she's laughing in a healthy way now, and that's what matters to Phil. Even before her sickness had her giggling at phantoms, she was a kid born to laugh. In her earliest photos, baby Melanie flashed grins that could ignite a pile of wet kelp. Somehow, in the cosmic crapshoot of heredity, she dodged both her mother's and her father's grim tendency to find a single tiny cloud in an otherwise sunny sky and stand shivering in its shade. Phil scratches his head at the memory of his son and daughter-in-law. Those two could suck the joy out of Mardi Gras. Even at her craziest, Melanie never loses her charm. Not in Phil's eyes.

"Come on," he says. "I'll buy you lunch at Ethereal." This is his idea of parenting. Melanie cannot resist the Ethereal Eatery. It's the last of the New Agey, old-Homer restaurants in town, now staffed by neo-hippie twenty-somethings. She loves the sheer goofiness of the name and the dreadlocked college kids cooking curried enchiladas and Thai-style pizzas for American heartland tourists. Vaguely foreign-sounding cuisine is the very white town's nod to diversity.

It puts her in better spirits. "Great. You go grab a booth before the tourists snatch them all. I'll meet you there in a few minutes." She waves her phone at him. "Gotta call Mom first. You know how she hates to be disappointed."

Phil knows all too well that his daughter-in-law cannot stand even the slightest setback to her expectations. He and Sandy did not part friends.

"Give her my love," he says.

Melanie snorts. "Funny, Pops."

Before she can dial her mother, her phone rings. She apparently recognizes the incoming number and answers cheerfully in a way that tells Phil it's someone her own age. He's got his coat on and is almost out the door when he hears her say, "No, silly, you can't get STDs from oral sex. Trust me."

Oh, good. This is *exactly* what he needs now.

*　*　*

At the Ethereal Eatery, Phil slides into the last available booth, trying not to think about his granddaughter's self-assured dispensation of inaccurate sex advice. The place is indeed mobbed with tourists, as reliable each summer as clouds and rain and returning salmon. Not the cruise ship folks with their identifying badges or bracelets; they get overfed like house pets onboard and shop only for T-shirts and mugs. This is mostly the road-weary Winnebago and rental car crowd.

There is also a young, obviously local couple sitting at a two-top by the big window facing the street. They're wearing Carhartt bibs, plaid flannel shirts, and brown Xtratufs of their own. They both have their heads down low over the table, and for a moment Phil thinks they're a couple of the town's many fundamentalist Christians giving thanks for their mochas and avocado toast. Then Joni the waitress brings their beverages, and they sit up. A cell phone lies face up on the table before each of them, the screens radiant. They've been praying all right, but to newer gods than Jesus.

Phil recognizes the boy—the kid's dad operates the sling gantry at the boatyard—but Phil hasn't seen the kid since he was in high school. He looks like a lot of the twenty-somethings he sees around town these days, home from college and looking for work. Or not.

Ingrid—Phil's battle-hardened high school principal—says that, given the lack of jobs in a place this small, there are only three kinds of kids that age in town: the ones who never managed to leave; the ones who left but found the outside world a lot less "snuggy" (Ingrid's word) and retreated home; and outsiders there to sell dope to the first two groups.

Phil would bet both testicles that this couple is from the second category and have nestled into an apartment over the boy's parents' garage, eating out of Mom and Dad's refrigerator and smoking now-legal weed between bouts of youthful humping. Really, blessed with that kind of setup, who looks for work? Seeing them makes him wonder if Melanie will ever find a life that passes for normal, even around there.

Through the front window he sees her pedal up in the still-falling drizzle and dismount. There's a bike rack alongside the building, but she parks hers in the middle of the sidewalk, determined, he supposes, to prove to him just how larcenous his beloved town has become. Her heavy clogs and big, stiff raincoat make her lumber like an astronaut. As she sets the kickstand, he catches a glimpse of her small silver-spangled face inside the rain hood, and asks himself once again whether a parent who presented his own son with a life apparently not worth living is the best candidate to steer the next generation straight.

Just as Melanie turns for the door, her bike falls over and slams against the tempered plate glass window of the restaurant with a nerve-jouncing blast that nearly launches the young couple out of their chairs. Every head in the place turns. Melanie looks down at her bike, then through the window at everyone inside watching her. She smiles, but Phil can tell that her mind is whirling. She can deal with one, maybe two small problems at a time. The stolen boots and her wet feet may have maxed her out today. He braces for her reaction.

Melanie leaves the bike where it lies on the sidewalk, walks in, pulls back the rain hood, and brays, "Has everyone heard the good news?" All eyes are on her. "With luck, none of us will get what we really deserve!"

Her maniacal outburst worries him, yet he finds the message comforting. Apparently, most of the tourists do too. They go back to their Korean chimichangas, their vegan fajitas. Girls with Melanie's punk trappings are probably not all that unusual in the cities these people come from, Phil muses. And they're getting more common here too. But Joni gives him a stern-waitress look, suggesting that Homer is not the kind of town where people shout cryptic pronouncements at full volume inside restaurants. He waves Melanie over to his booth. She takes the seat opposite and wriggles out of the bulky rubber raincoat.

He's about to bring up the concept of "inside" voices when he realizes that's a term that might mean something very different for someone with Melanie's brain. Luckily, just then Ingrid walks in. His Ingrid. Six feet tall and brilliantly blond, she's a former cross-country ski champ, and still frighteningly fit. Her idea of a relaxing leisure-time activity is ice climbing. Not a Norse goddess exactly, but as close to one as he'll ever get, and he knows it.

Since Melanie arrived in town, he and Ingrid have not been spending nearly as much time together as he'd like. Ingrid claims she doesn't want to intrude on his attempt at parenting. She's thirty-nine and dates Phil instead of men her own age, men who—unlike her—might want to start a family. She says she's "letting the clock run out." That's her business, of course. And in any case he doesn't want her to play the hated surrogate mom role. He's seen the family mayhem those situations have precipitated among friends in town with so-called "blended" marriages.

Melanie spots Ingrid and shouts, "Hi, Ingrid! Join us? The old guy's buying!"

"Ooh," Ingrid says, "if Phil's paying, slide over." She drops into the booth at Melanie's side. "I don't suppose they serve steak and lobster at lunch?"

Melanie waves a menu. "The 'halibut with chipotle-tamarind pesto on a bed of massaged kale' is the most expensive lunch thing."

Phil can see he's going to be the straight man at this performance. He doesn't mind. It's good to see Melanie making Ingrid her partner in comedy, and he forcefully resists the vision of the three of them together for anything more permanent than a lunch. Ingrid will have no part of it. He's not sure Melanie would either. It's quite possible he alone nurtures such domestic fantasies.

Joni comes to take their order and compliments Melanie on her neck ink. Wispy blue tree branches curl out of her raggy sweater and reach up her neck toward her many earrings. Butterflies and tiny birds perch on the twig ends. Flattered, Melanie yanks the hem of the sweater up and pins it to her collarbone with her chin, revealing to Joni—and everyone in the restaurant—the tattooed tree trunk growing out of her pink brassiere. When she stuffs four fingers under each cup and starts lifting, Phil is sure they're going to see the tree's root system, and much more. Ingrid gently tugs Melanie's sweater back down, and the two of them crack up.

Melanie howls, "He thought I was going to do it! He did! Admit it, Pops!"

Ingrid says, "*I* certainly thought you were." More laughter.

Melanie's discharge instructions included a caveat: "Coupled with the sometimes impulsive behavior common to her illness, Melanie has also learned to get attention by acting inappropriately."

Phil offered to pay the facility extra if they told him something he *didn't* already know.

Melanie barks like a harbor seal. "Ark! Ark! Your face! Oh, God. Hah!"

"Hah," he says, and sips his coffee, happy that, however inappropriate Melanie's stunt, this was at least intentional humor. Her laughter is not the deranged cackle he's heard too often, and it tickles him to see the two women in his life having a good time together. They eat their lunch without further theater, Melanie still snickering to herself and muttering, "I totally got you, Pops."

She finishes her food and says, "Thanks for the grub. I gotta go to Kundalini."

Phil momentarily thinks he and Ingrid will finally have some time to themselves, but Ingrid stands to let Melanie out of the booth and says, "I have to go too, Phil. School's never out for a principal. Thanks for lunch." She leans and gives him a peck on the cheek that doesn't actually touch his skin. Her hands remain at her sides. No contact at all.

Ruefully, Phil understands. In her years working at various Alaskan high schools, Ingrid has seen too many problematic teenagers shipped up from the Lower 48 by one divorced and overwhelmed parent to live in Alaska with the kid's other, soon-to-be-overwhelmed parent—or, more and more often recently, a grandparent. She knows what the odds are of that working, and she's steering clear. He'd like to say that he can't blame her. But the distance she's putting between them leaves a heavy taste on his tongue.

Or maybe that's just all the cumin.

* * *

Mid-afternoon, he's standing at his living room window, watching the Coastal Roofing Company estimator stow an extension ladder on his truck and wondering if there's some way to get Ingrid to ask Melanie about her apparent sexual expertise, when a Homer Police cruiser rolls up his driveway. There's a shock of blue hair visible in the back seat. If asked, Phil would say he thinks it's fair to assume that nobody wants to see their granddaughter being unloaded from a police car. He assures himself that if this involved drugs, the police wouldn't be giving her a ride home. The two uniformed cops exchange howdies with the roofer, then trundle Melanie to the front door. One is Officer Ted Coover. Ted won the local king salmon derby last year and came in third the year before. Phil knows him and his boat well. They're not really friends, but Phil thinks they could be, given the chance. The other cop is a stranger: young, shaved head, tiny ears, concrete neck. Phil gets the picture: high school wrestler finally living his dream in law enforcement.

Phil opens his front door. Before he can even ask, Ted Coover says, "Shoplifting."

Shrugging theatrically, Melanie pulls her spangled lips back in a toothy rictus. She looks like a hyena, if hyenas went in for tongue studs.

Ted tells him she tried to steal a pair of expensive pants from Seaside Sally's, the closest thing to a boutique in town. That is strange, given that Melanie wears nothing but shredded jeans and thrift shop sweaters so stretched out they look like they've been used as purse seines for salmon. But there's really no guessing what she'll do next. With her earlier phone conversation still echoing in his brain, he's relieved that it's only shoplifting and not soliciting. Who knows what those voices in her head are suggesting?

"Leather," Ted says and grimaces.

"Leather, Ted?"

"The pants."

"Are they pressing charges?"

Ted shakes his head. "That new school principal was there. Tall, nice-looking blond? She talked to the owner, smoothed things out, explained your girl's problems."

Phil should be delighted that Ingrid came to Melanie's rescue, but all he can hear is "your girl's problems." Is that the talk of the town now? He feels his blood warming.

The young cop—his name tag reads Officer Durez—smirks. "You know, sir, we can't give a kid a pass on something like this more than once."

Phil's pulse rushes. He'd love to wipe that look off Durez's face. But the guy is thirty years younger and wearing a badge. Never mind the taser, pistol, and nightstick. He decides to defer to the better part of valor. He turns to Ted Coover. "Thanks, Ted. I'll handle it."

The look on Ted's face says, Phil, what the fuck are you doing, trying to raise a troubled, drug-abusing girl? At your age?

Phil hopes his own face says, You're six months past due on last winter's boat storage, Ted. And I haven't made a peep because I know about your wife's MS. And because that's the kind of town we are here.

When the police leave, he turns to Melanie. All he can say is, "Leather?"

Melanie crumples, truly defeated for the first time in the weeks she's been there. She sobs and chokes and makes horrible injured-animal noises. But what shakes him most isn't the sound as much as the shape of her mouth, which, through his own watery eyes, distorts into a gaping hole in her heavily pierced face. What is it he's seeing?

*　*　*

When Phil was Melanie's age, he lived in a small industrial city in southern Michigan. One summer he caught a black bass in the fetid local river behind the radiator plant. Coming from water that generally produced nothing but stunted bullheads and puny perch, the gamefish was a rarity, a trophy worth mounting. His family couldn't afford taxidermy, of course. So he cut the fish's head off and set it out to dry in the summer sun, high on the roof to keep the rats off it. When the flies and maggots had done their jobs, and nothing remained except the desiccated skin stretched over the skull beneath, he brought it down and varnished it, coat after coat, until it glowed like a live wet fish again. Then he glued glass marbles into the empty eye sockets and painted them with glossy model airplane enamel: yellow rings around big black pupils.

He mounted the bass head on a wooden plaque and proudly hung it on his bedroom wall, and the fish glared out at the room with those bulging painted eyes, its mouth gaping in silent laughter. The sun-hardened tongue pointed like an accusing finger, saying, "Look what you've done to me!" And Phil began to see it for what it was: the face of madness. Something he feared more than anything in the world.

*　*　*

Melanie is laughing again. Too hard. Too loud. Tears demolish her abundant makeup. Her eyes are frantic. Phil says, "Jesus, Mel, I'm trying here, honey. I'm not good at this, but I'm trying."

"Me too," she laughs. "I'm trying too. But I'm not good at this either!"

He gathers her into a hug, her cold ear metal pressed against his neck. Through the wild strands of her very blue hair, he sees her spinning wheel, her little wooden bench, her basket of yarn balls under their living room window, looking like an illustration of another time, another world.

Her phone rings and she pulls away and sniffs, "I've got to take this," and slips down the hall to her room, murmuring into the phone and leaving him standing there alone once more.

Outside the window, the roofer's truck backs down the driveway. The Homer Police cruiser remains parked out front. Officers Coover and Durez are filling out their report. And on some level, it comforts Phil to know that they are doing everything they can to keep this town the kind of place he hopes it still is.

Angels, Jellies, and Squid

Every night that summer the regulars at the Unisea danced, glowing Cyalume sticks dangling from their necks on fishing line like radioactive green amulets. Some of the cod fleet used the things to attract fish to the pots, and the whole island was flooded with them. Julie nursed her overpriced vodka and watched the slime-line college brats, the Filipino dock workers, the Mexican and Vietnamese kitchen staff from cannery housing—and the fishermen, of course, in every size and shape—gyrating on the dance floor like luminescent sea creatures writhing in deep ocean darkness.

The ugly confrontation on the trawler that morning still had her feeling like she might rip her own skin off and attack the next man that slit his eyes her way. She could see herself peeled and lunging, all muscles and blood. She was aware that a bar full of drunk fishermen on a rock halfway between Anchorage and Kamchatka was probably not the best place to burn an evening onshore. Not in her mood. And she reminded herself that she took up boxing in the first place to learn to control her sometimes murderous anger. But there was nothing much else to do in the middle of the night on a small island in the middle of the Pacific—however romantic that sounded. No tiki bars on this one, no honeymoon lagoons. Just a couple thousand men moving dead fish around in the constant Bering Sea wind and rain. And a handful of women "too adventurous for their own damn good," as her father put it.

The bar band was covering '80s hits at permanent-hearing-loss volume, a dizzying roar in her sea-weary ears. She was thinking about having one more drink when an enormous young fisherman with a bandana cinched piratically around his bushy black hair loomed over her. He had a dozen glow sticks strung on a line around his neck, fanned out across his chest like a green piano keyboard.

"Dance?" he howled through the freight train beat and took a sudden step back to catch his balance, clearly bombed. He couldn't have been much over twenty. Must have weighed 300 pounds, Popeye forearms bulging from rolled-up sleeves, plaid flannel chest as wide as a truck grille. He wore wraparound Ray-Bans despite the bar's thick darkness, his glow sticks reflecting in the black plastic lenses like the wavering headlights of an unavoidable head-on coming her way. He was apparently too drunk to notice her haircut, her attitude. No gaydar at all. That was rare. And a blessing of sorts.

Julie shook her head, shouted, "No, thank you!" and tensed for the response. After three years working on the boats, she would've bet $100 on either *dyke*, *bitch*, or *cunt*. Maybe some combination of the three. To her amazement, the guy bowed like a Jane Austen dandy, turned, and plowed off into the dancers, clearly even drunker than she'd thought. She had to smile. First time in days.

The goofy encounter took the edge off, unlocked her jaw. She was reasonably certain nothing that good was going to happen there again this night. She threw back the lemony ice-melt in her glass, stood to leave. The bartender, a dreadlocked Jamaican named Eddie, caught her eye. He pointed to her empty glass, arched his caterpillar eyebrows, and nodded enticingly.

She shook her head, pushed back her chair.

He mouthed, "Thank you!" and gave her a brilliant Caribbean smile.

Not for the first time, she thought how nice it would be to work there in the bar instead of on the ships. Bartenders were paid to be friendly. Fishermen were paid by the weight of their catch. Being the person who told them what kind of fish and how many they were allowed to kill never made you any friends on the boats.

Having a vagina didn't help. Having no interest in sharing it with men only added to the problem.

Outside the building the air thrummed with the twenty-four-hour dock work. Gantry cranes clanked on the loading piers. A ship's horn moaned from the mists. She zipped her jacket against the chill, although it was summer and the first windless night in three boat-tossing weeks. The sea-damp air touched her face, thick with fish and brine, fish and diesel, and fish and more fish. A wisp of pot smoke tickled her nostrils. She inhaled and tasted it on her tongue. That was another thing—along with sleep, decent meals, healthy exercise, and any semblance of civility—you had to give up as a fisheries observer. Well, if somebody didn't keep an eye on these guys, there would soon be nothing left swimming out there but jellies and squid.

She felt like she had her shoes on the wrong feet, but understood it was the vodka and the residual sea swells still rolling in her brain. Not to mention the wearying stress from the past few days on the problematic trawler. There was no point in going up to her room above the bar. She would doze in the lull between sets, only to be launched upright in bed minutes later by another thunderous bass line. The '80s. Her mother's music. Jesus. Who thought that shit was worth resurrecting?

It was a good time to walk. Nothing moved on the gravel harbor road except the third-shift forklifts darting like black and yellow wasps between the docks and the canneries, endless pallets of fish-filled totes in their steel arms. She hadn't gone ten feet when one of the island's many feral cats staggered past, its incest-addled brain giving it a shaky gait that made her own clumsy steps seem balletic by comparison.

"Kitty, kitty," she sang to it, but it lurched on, each step a crazy, knee-locked stab at the gravel beneath it. Spend enough time on this island and you'll grow extra toes and walk like that too. One more season and she was out for good. One more. Maybe two, tops.

She wandered down the waterfront road under sodium lights, hot ash white against the Alaskan midnight gloaming. A dozen refrigerated trailers lined the ocean side of the road like gigantic sandbags set there to ward off a tsunami, an electric drone emanating from their always-running compressors. At the end of the trailers a garbage-reeking dumpster sat in a cone of light under a streetlamp, the heavy steel lid propped open. Four enormous eagles perched in a row on it, erect as nuns at Communion. They rolled their fierce yellow eyes her way but didn't budge.

"Really, guys?" she said. "The symbol of democracy? Dumpster diving? Look at yourselves."

Talk about self-awareness. She was chatting with brain-damaged cats and carrion birds. Shit. She needed to set her feet on land attached to a continent. Any continent. And soon.

She turned away from the dumpster to find three guys gushing from a doorway as if the building had vomited them out. They blundered into the street a few yards ahead, hanging onto each other, too high to even laugh about it. Julie stood up straight as they caught sight of her.

"Oh, dear," one of them said. She knew the voice, knew the toothy rodent face. The attitude. Skinny guy with an Aussie accent. "It's little Miss Fisheries Observer!" He stepped closer. "Or should I say Mister?"

Great. Two thousand men on this island and she had to deal with this one for the second time today. She knew better than to try to reason with him. It hadn't worked on the boat earlier that afternoon—when he'd been sober. She just glared, something smoldering under her ribs.

His two buddies were not from the trawler, didn't know what the beef was. One of them said, "Dink, what's up?" his voice edgy from something more potent than alcohol. Modern chemistry at work. "Who's the chick?"

The Aussie moved closer, waiting for her to step back. She didn't budge.

"It's the dyke from the boat. Real cunt," he said. "Bitch fucked up our whole week."

There it was. The trifecta. Impressive.

The skinny runt raised his hands to shove her, planted them on her chest. Squeezed. She knocked them wide with her forearms and gave him four knuckles to the windpipe. He went to his knees, clutching his throat. She landed two quick jabs to his nose. The contact electrified her. The look on his face. She planted her foot in the gravel and put her weight into a roundhouse hook that hurled him onto his back.

Barely aware that the eagles were panic-flapping away, she dropped one knee onto his chest and pounded him. No style now. No discipline. Everything she'd learned at the gym lost to the venting rage. That's what these guys did to you. Made you take control. And then lose control. A cut opened under one eye. His nose spurted. She tasted his blood on her lips but kept hitting. God knows how long she would've kept it up.

One of his pals shouted to the other one, "Jesus, man, do something! She's going to kill the stupid bastard. Pull her off him!"

The other one grabbed the collar of her jacket with one hand, her belt with his other. Julie was still swinging wildly as he lifted her off the ground and pitched her into the dumpster.

* * *

She dreamt of being lost in an unfamiliar building, all hallways and stairwells, the air dense with the stench of wet garbage. She wandered there for what seemed like hours, trying locked doors. Rain began to fall on her face, waking her out of the dream. She found herself on a bed of bulging black Hefty bags, head throbbing and thick. The endless droning of the refrigeration units drilled her ears.

For a moment she thought she was still on one of the ships—the rancid odors, the noise—but there was none of the ceaseless motion of the sea. She squinted into the streetlamp overhead, raised one hand to shade her eyes and felt a gash on her forehead where she'd hit the edge of the dumpster going in. Her hand came away with blood. Her own now. When she tried to stand to look out over the rim of the box, pain shot from her left ankle, the other point of contact with the steel walls. Her leg buckled and she collapsed onto the wet garbage bags. Well, she'd been wanting to get out of the job and off the fishing boats. A broken leg would make that happen. But first she needed to get out of this box before the truck came to empty it. Ending up in the island's landfill under a couple tons of sopping garbage almost sounded like a step up from fisheries observer. But still.

She was about to try climbing out when she heard the crunch of gravel, footsteps approaching. "Hey!" she yelled. "Anybody out there?"

The face of an angel appeared over the edge of the dumpster. Long, straight red hair damp with rainwater, trailing out from under a black knitted watch cap. Eyes that shone green as gems in the lamplight. Freckles across the nose, a dimple in each pale cheek. A vision so feminine it hurt Julie's heart.

The angel spoke: "What the hell are you doing in the goddamn garbage?"

Things were looking up.

* * *

They got home to the angel Margaret's house from the emergency room at 4:00 in the morning, Julie's leg in a cast, her head bandaged. It was a tiny place on the beach, strapped to the ground with thick steel cables stretching across the roof and anchored to concrete piers buried deep in the earth. Margaret insisted Julie stay with her until it was clear that she didn't have a concussion. Never mind what the doctors said. Julie didn't resist the idea of staying in a real house, sleeping in a bed that did not have Duran Duran blasting up through the floor beneath it.

Margaret's house was a museum of crap. The woman collected things of no measurable value and was a slave to genres. She collected egg cups, measuring cups, teacups. Safety pins, hairpins, hat pins. One wall of her living room was covered with old postcards. A picture of Niagara Falls sent to someone in Oregon. Mt. Rushmore inscribed to somebody's aunt in Florida. A Manitoba pike-fishing lodge addressed to a loved one in El Paso. "Fishing is bad, insects worse. Miss you so much." The whole house smelled of bread baking.

"I like your house," Julie said, feeling the pain meds softening the inside of her skull. Oddly, the knuckles on her right hand hurt worse than the gash in her forehead or the fractured left tibia. The doctor had X-rayed her hand and declared it sound. Just bruises.

Margaret held the wounded knuckles against her cheek. "What you did wasn't a great idea," she said gently.

"I used to box," Julie said, the words sounding sleepy and wet.

"Box?" Margaret said. "Why?"

Julie hesitated. It seemed like so long ago. What was she going to say to this perfect, beautiful stranger? That she had four older, brutal brothers, an equally mean mother, and a father who'd given up trying to domesticate any of them long before Julie was even born? "I'm not sure," she said. "Can I get a shower?"

She wanted to get the garbage odor out of her hair, her skin. And anything else about this night that she could wash away. But she wasn't supposed to soak the bandage on her forehead, nor the cast on her ankle. Realistically, she couldn't lift that leg into the bathtub if she wanted to anyhow. She mumbled that she could give herself a sponge bath. Again, Margaret insisted on helping. Such an angel. She put a blue plastic tarp down on the living room floor, undressed Julie and taped her cast inside a white kitchen trash bag, washed her with warm soapy water and a soft cloth. All over. Again, Julie didn't fight it. She stood naked in the middle of the tarp, woozy with meds and exhaustion, the vinyl sticky under her bare feet. Margaret's hand between her legs. It was the first gentle thing she'd felt in months. They made love. Slept till noon.

* * *

Margaret didn't own a car. She rode her bike to the elementary school where she taught third grade. When she needed groceries, she'd call Minh's Taxi: *$5.00 Anywhere on the Island!* Mrs. Minh got out of Vietnam when Saigon fell in the '70s. Been there on the island since the '80s. Her children and grandchildren ran the pizza place, a building maintenance company, at least two massage parlors. She drove a Dodge Caravan with her great-grandchildren playing in the back—toddlers and infants of indeterminate ages and gender. Julie learned not to expect Mrs. Minh to smile. The children, on the other hand, never stopped.

The angel Margaret grew vegetables in barrels on her porch. She ate off washable china plates and cups—nothing disposable. Ever. Not a spray can in the house. Because the island had recycling bins only for glass and paper, she had a special suitcase for clear plastic containers, which she took to Anchorage as checked baggage each

Christmas and spring break. Her walls were covered with calendars from the Nature Conservancy, Planned Parenthood, Doctors without Borders. She fed the feral cats on her front porch with the most expensive canned food the Alaska Commercial store sold. When possible, she captured them and paid to have them neutered. She was off school for the summer but volunteered at the island's small library, reading to children, bringing books to old people at the senior center. Julie wanted to be that good one day.

She learned that Margaret's husband had died and left her their house in San Francisco. Margaret sold it and used some of the almost unbelievable sum of cash to put her two daughters through college. Moved to the Aleutians. Bought the little house. She apparently invested the rest. Julie didn't understand the financial talk but wanted to be that independent. That smart too.

She called the Groundfish Fisheries office in Anchorage and took a medical leave.

* * *

All summer, Julie read the novels that Margaret also collected. Cranked up Margaret's CDs to drown out the constant storms and the endless rain. Margaret's musical tastes ran to folksy shit—banjos, for Christ's sake—but it was better than the wind. They cooked three meals a day together, slept huddled like mice in a grassy nest. She was happy to be inside the house instead of on the heaving deck of a trawler or long-liner crashing through mountains of hard green seawater in some of the worst weather in the world. Happy to live with an angel. Who wouldn't be?

Midsummer Margaret got word that silver salmon were schooling at the mouth of Pilot Creek. She called Minh's Taxi. They piled fishing tackle and a Coleman cooler into the van, shoving two long spinning rods in among the little Minhs. Old Mrs. Minh frowned more than usual. The children laughed. At the creek Julie stumbled over the rocks and mud with her cast in a plastic bag again. She screamed like an idiot every time she hooked one of the milling salmon. She and Margaret knelt together in the mud and clubbed the fish to death with rocks, slit their gills to bleed them out. The violence thrilled Julie more than she wanted to think about. When it was time to go home, Margaret called the taxi on her cell.

Mrs. Minh was not happy about their mud-and-blood-splattered condition. She made them take their pants off before they got in the van. The children found that hilarious. Margaret gave Mrs. Minh a huge tip. Mrs. Minh might have smiled. Hard to tell.

At home they canned the fish in Kerr jars. The pressure canner rattled for exactly 110 minutes while they took a shower together and had a sex nap. For two days after that the house smelled like the town in Maine where Julie had spent her sophomore year of high school. Lobster shacks and bait stores. Different oceans, a continent away. The familiar seafood scent was comforting.

On rare clear days she sat on the porch steps in the blessed sun and talked to the shaky cats while Margaret fussed with her kale, cucumbers, radishes. Julie listened to the ocean, to the ships. It was the pollock-trawling season—she remembered that for some reason—yellowfin sole and sablefish too. Who was keeping track of the catch? she wondered, but only briefly. Margaret brought her a vodka with fresh mint leaves. What fishermen? What fish?

Although the weather was hideous most days, the pervasive gloom couldn't faze an angel. Margaret made Julie exercise, cajoled her into walking on the beach in the misting drizzle, Julie's cast dragging a furrow in the damp sand between the two rows of holes punched by her crutches. They picnicked in fog as thick as oatmeal. On days when the rain rode the wind horizontally and it was too much even for Margaret, they stayed inside and watched movies.

Margaret had shelves of DVDs, mostly cable TV series. Hundreds of individual discs and box sets. They ate dinner in front of the TV, binge-watching episode after episode. Margaret let Julie work the remote. Julie loved to push the button on Play All. They binge-watched *Mad Men* and drank old-fashioneds. They watched *Justified* and drank straight bourbon. They watched *Deadwood* and learned to swear horribly, agreeing that it was "an unmitigated cock-sucking tragedy" that the show had been cancelled after just three seasons. They only disagreed once, and briefly. Margaret said that—compared to Ian McShane—Timothy Oliphant was a pussy.

Julie said, "You'd fuck him in a heartbeat, and you know it."

Margaret laughed.

Angels don't fight. They just won't.

In late August a continuous chain of gigantic low-pressure systems moved in from the Bering Sea. Storm after monstrous storm bashed the island. The school semester began and Margaret went back to work. Each morning she pedaled off on her bike in orange rubber rain pants and matching coat, the hood cinched under her chin. Julie watched her go and moved back inside the house, looked at the clock, picked up a book to read. Looked at the clock again.

Margaret was gone all day now. Rain hosed the windows. The wind pushed the walls in closer. The cats showed up on the porch begging for meals, soaked and shivering, hopelessly bedraggled. The wind wanted to tear the house off its foundation, toss it in the sea. Julie felt the framing straining against the steel cables binding the place to the beach, every joist and rafter groaning on the gusts. The clutter of Margaret's collections leaned in on her.

With school back in session Margaret's book club started up again and her quilting group resumed. She began to stay late at school some afternoons. Meetings. She never said what kind.

Julie's cast came off and she was walking without her crutches. But there was nowhere to walk, the beach lost in the maelstrom of wind and foaming surf. Shredded seaweed plastered the back of the house like slick green wallpaper. The road to town was an obstacle course of ankle-deep puddles, forklifts careening around them, drivers blinded by the rain. She stayed indoors and walked around the kitchen table on her healed leg. Drank alone.

One morning Margaret asked Julie if she wanted to join her and some of the teachers for dinner at Minh's pizzeria that night. "You need to get out of the house," she said.

The pity made Julie's knuckles ache for something to punch. "You're right," she said. Heard the bitchiness in her voice. Couldn't stop herself. "But not with that bunch of simps." She'd met Margaret's peers, the other elementary school teachers, the first week of school. Everyone so nice it made her ass twitch. Those women generously gave Margaret's switch-hitting a pass. But they looked at Julie like she was some kind of malevolent succubus there to feed on angel flesh.

Margaret wouldn't rise to the bait. "Okay, honey," she said. "I won't be late."

Living with an angel was not always everything it was cracked up to be.

* * *

One gale-battered afternoon, a sudden hollow metal banging made Julie look up from her reading and out the window. A wind-tossed aluminum skiff tumbled, gunwale over gunwale, down the center of the road. The two-note booming seemed to be saying, "Wake up! Wake up! Wake up!"

That same day Margaret called to say her bike had a flat tire. She got a ride home—late—with the new school principal, her bike strapped to his car-top carriers. He was a tall, partly Native man. Very handsome. His name was Russ.

Julie stood on the porch and tried not to glare. She felt the fury rising. It took all her will to ignore it. "Hello," she said, and it sounded like the stupidest thing anyone had ever uttered.

"I invited Russ to stay for dinner," Margaret shouted up to her through the wind and rain as she wrestled her bike off his Subaru's roof racks. "I wanted you two to meet."

"We already met," Julie snarled, "at the orientation event." Regretted it. But just a little.

"Sure," Russ said, pretending he hadn't heard the acid in her voice. He stood at the foot of the porch stairs holding an umbrella over his head. He let Margaret handle the bike herself.

Smart, Julie thought. He already knows what she likes, how she is. How does he know that?

She watched him watching Margaret's perfect, rubber-clad ass as she climbed the steps and onto the porch with the bike.

That tire didn't look very flat.

Margaret gave her a friendly arm pinch as she walked by. No kiss. "Pop us some beers?" All smiles.

They had planned to watch *Orange Is the New Black* with dinner. Now they had to eat at the table. Margaret put out cloth napkins. Julie wanted to tear them to shreds. Wanted to tear *her* to shreds.

Halfway through dinner, apropos of nothing, Julie said to Russ, "Margaret says you're Native." Russ had his head down, working on his lasagna.

Margaret rolled her eyes at Julie, silently mouthed, "What the fuck?"

Russ was silent for a moment before he answered. "One quarter Aleut," he said, looking up, smiling, "on my mother's side."

Julie got the feeling he wanted her to know he was from a marginalized subculture too. Straight people did that sometimes. "Margaret's part lesbian," she said, "on *her* mother's side. Fifty percent."

Russ laughed. There was so much confidence in his laughter that Julie knew he'd already fucked Margaret. After-school meetings? Sure. Technically, two people and a bed was a meeting.

When Russ left, they had their first real fight. Their last. Margaret insisting it was all Julie's imagination. There was nothing going on with her and Russ. Julie managed not to hit her. Barely. What kind of asshole would punch an angel?

She stomped out, walked all the way to the Grand Aleutian in the constant rain, and got a room.

*   *   *

The Pacific gray cod season opened in the Gulf of Alaska in September. The weather sucked, but no more than usual. Thirty-knot winds. Seas eight to ten feet. Julie puked for the first half day as they steamed out to the fishing grounds. But then she was all right. She was better than all right. The ankle was surprisingly strong. And her knuckles had finally stopped aching too, though she reminded herself never to hit anyone that hard again bare-fisted. Even the head wound had healed nicely. There was a small jagged scar. But a person would have to get very close to see it, and she was not going to let that happen again anytime soon.

As the ship sliced through the heavy seas, she leaned on the aft rail, inhaling diesel exhaust and watching the prop wash churning and foaming behind the huge double screws below. She thought about letting her hair grow out and combing it down over her forehead. Just as she had thought about going home, back to the gym and training, back into the ring. People paid good money to see two women beat the shit out of each other. She thought about doing something—anything—on solid earth, miles from the nearest salt-water. She thought about it all.

Then she thought, fuck it. The oceans need an angel too.

So, Kenny the Sheetrocker Sends for His Girl

Word around camp is Kenny the Sheetrocker's flying his girl in from Anchorage. Nobody's ever heard of anything like that—not out here in Quinhagak or Emmonak or Kalskag or Lower Kalskag—or wherever the hell we are. Believe me, these places all start to look alike from under a hard hat.

The point is you just don't bring your girl to the job. Not if you have any self-respect. Or decency. I mean, you have to *work* with these guys.

It's bad enough the rest of us haven't seen our wives or girlfriends for however many weeks we've been out here building this school so that six college graduates will have jobs teaching twenty-seven local kids algebra and commas and shit that even big-city kids will never need, never mind the poor bastards stuck out here in the wettest, buggiest swamp in Alaska. But it'll be a lot worse for Kenny, having every slob in camp standing on the airstrip waiting to run their eyeballs over his girl.

At first I thought Floyd, the job super, started the rumor to bust everyone's balls. I mean, it's only been like two weeks since the inspector signed off on the electrical and let us start the sheetrocking. And that's when Kenny showed up. Two weeks ago. And he has to see his girl? Already?

My own girlfriend Marla—very smart, reads a lot of magazines— would say there might be "trust issues" in that relationship. If that's the problem, I feel for Kenny. I really do.

The plane is coming in late tonight, and given the limited entertainment options out here, you can bet the whole crew will be waiting at the airport to see if she shows up.

Airport. That's a stretch. The landing strip is dirt and ice gone to mud at this time of year, and the terminal is an unpainted wooden shack. Inside there's one local gal with long black pigtails and one wrecked-out white woman who looks like she's lived out here in the bush since the last Ice Age. The whole building smells like the inside of a wet boot. There's no TSA checking departing passengers because nobody with half a heart would mess up anyone's chance to get out of this place.

Incoming is a different matter. The village is legally dry. That means a bottle of Kirkland vodka that sells for $13 in Anchorage goes for $130 here. So now the village public safety officer is waiting on the strip for the plane with the rest of us.

Somehow it feels good, waiting for Kenny's girl to arrive. It's the first really new thing I can remember happening for months. When you're a laborer on bush jobs, you're there the day the dozer scrapes the willows off the tundra. And a year later, after the carpet layers and painters have all gone back to the big city and decent pizzas, you're still there wiping the dust off the last door frame, the last windowsill. That feels like job security these days. But so do consecutive life sentences.

Of course, now and then you get time off to go home. If you want it. Personally, I've lost interest since the day Marla called to tell me somebody broke into our apartment and stole all my guns and our flat screen, and I jumped on the next plane out to see if she was okay. Turns out it was Marla's wasted brother and his smack-addict pals. And maybe Marla knew something about that, since the cops said there was no sign of forced entry. We had a big fight, and okay, maybe I raised my voice a little—some of those guns had been my father's, and that TV was a plasma screen—but no way was I "verbally abusive."

She said I was just like every other man in her fucked-up life—her exact words—and then she left. Every other man? Really? Every one?

I guess I'll never know. She won't even pick up when I call now. Which is why I haven't taken any time off for a while, and maybe why Kenny flying his girl in is such a big deal for me.

*   *   *

The whole camp's out on the airstrip now. Virgil and Kyle the electricians, Red the carpenter foreman and his crew, the two rat-faced sprinkler guys from Wasilla. Everybody's smoking or chewing 100 miles an hour, like they've just heard that the liberals are finally going to completely outlaw tobacco everywhere in the world. Floyd, the boss, sits in his rig, windows rolled up against the flies, looking at us and shaking his head and smiling like he knows something we don't. Which makes me wonder if Kenny's girl really is on that plane.

We can hear the engine somewhere up there in clouds so thick and dark they're like a huge wet blanket somebody threw over this place. And we're so wound up you'd think the plane's flying in a vaccine just in time to save us from some disease we don't even know the name of. And maybe it is.

Jules the plumber, a big Jerry Garcia–looking guy with hair down to his ass and a beard as black as his fingernails, has spent the afternoon unclogging the urinal pipe in the Porta Potti—nothing can stop some guys from spitting chew into a urinal—and now he's actually nibbling those nails. You'd think a plumber would know better. He mutters something about Kenny's girl not showing up.

For some reason I say, "Oh, she'll be on the plane. I know it."

Jules pokes me with one toilet finger, says, "Twenty bucks it was Floyd screwing with our minds."

I don't even hesitate. "On," I say. "Twenty."

Look, I understand that betting on Kenny's girl is lame. I do. Maybe even evil. But I still show Jules my $20 bill. Which makes me wonder: if you know you're doing something ignorant, does that mean you're smart? Or more ignorant? Now *those* are the kinds of things they should be teaching the kids in this school. If we ever get the fucker built.

Of course Kenny's in a horrible spot now. If his girl *is* on the plane, he'll have to walk her to his truck with all the guys pretending they aren't eyeballing her while doing exactly that. And if she *isn't* on the plane? Then he's been punked so bad he won't be able to take a leak without some joker locking him in the john. Believe me, once you cinch a good nylon utility strap around a Porta Potti, whoever's in there won't be getting out for a while.

*   *   *

The plane has banked out of the clouds and is just touching down on the strip now, and Kenny's shifting from foot to foot and sucking on an American Spirit like he's going to inhale the whole thing: the paper, the tobacco, and the hot ash too.

I'm feeling kind of lucky compared to him, maybe even blessed. I know "laborer" doesn't sound like much, but there's a lot more to it than just lugging stuff off a truck and stacking it on the site. It takes certain skills. Out here, in places like this, I'm doing important work. I have to keep reminding myself of that.

It makes me sad that Marla never understood that. I thought we were doing okay. I thought *she* was doing okay. All those years of foster care, living on the streets, the crack, the oxy—over and done. We should have been golden with all that behind her.

Behind her? That was a bad choice of words. When I came through the door in Anchorage, worried sick—burglars? was she hurt?—what was behind her, right close behind her, was some guy named Wilby. Like the cops said, no forced entry. Wilby? What kind of a man is named Wilby?

The answer is, a man who does that to your wife while you're away working. *Working*, for Christ's sake! Nothing is sacred anymore.

I can't think about it now that the plane, a single-engine Otter, is sputtering to a stop in front of us. The wind kicks up the way it does out here, and the clouds split open, and the sun comes through like it's throwing a spotlight on the arrival of Kenny's girl. But the plane's windows are so lit up with glare we can't see in, can't tell if there are any passengers at all. Some days all the plane carries is the mail packet, a few cases of Coke and Mountain Dew for the village store. Maybe parts for somebody's outboard motor.

We watch the air-service kid walk straight to the cargo door and unlatch it. Maybe that's going to be it. All cargo today. Nobody on the plane. Poor Kenny.

Then the passenger door opens. First out is a nice old guy named Charlie, one of the village elders. He brought smoked fish to the job site one time and shared it with us like we're part of the tribe, not just a bunch of white guys from Anchorage making $40 an hour to hammer nails and push brooms. The cargo kid runs over and helps the old guy climb down the steps.

Next off is a big blond nurse from the village clinic. She's nice too—she stitched me up when I sliced my thumb with a drywall knife—but she's a little wide in the hips, and the guys call her Nurse Walrus. Guys can get like that out here. Nobody helps *her* down. She gives us all a stiff look and walks to the clinic truck. Then there's nobody for a minute. The passenger door is dark.

Jules the plumber holds out his hand for my 20. "Told you."

Poor Kenny's rocking heel to toe like one of those blow-up punching-bag dummies with sand in its butt and smiling like somebody's just punched him in the mouth and he wants to hang onto that smile because he knows it's his last one for the length of this job. Maybe ever.

Jules says, "Pay up, loser. The chick ain't on the plane."

I almost hand him the bill. Almost.

But then there she is. Kenny's girl.

She steps out the door and into the sunshine, holding down her skirt against the wind, and waits on the top step like she's a rock star looking out at her fans. Only this girl will never have a lot of fans. Not with that face. Pushed-up nose, mushy chin, little piggy eyes, lips like two Vienna sausages rubbing up against each other. Still, she came all the way from Anchorage to see Kenny. That's no small thing.

And neither is Kenny's girl.

"Jesus," a jerk behind me snorts. "Kenny paid money to fly *that* out here? He should've shipped her on the container barge."

I don't know why they get like this. I really don't.

But I'm happy that Kenny's not paying any attention anyway, because his girl has spotted him and she's waving. And now he's marching across the mud to help her down the steps because she's wearing shoes with heels like wood chisels. And now he's reaching for her hand. And now she's squeezing his hand and stepping down those stairs.

And now I do believe that they're going to kiss.

And they do. They kiss. Right there in front of everybody: the sparkies, the wood butchers, the sprinks, Floyd in his truck, the whole damn camp.

Honest to God—and I'm not just saying this because I made 20 bucks off that dumbass plumber—I truly think it's the most beautiful fucking thing I've ever seen.

I mean, why can't it always be like this?

Little Wing

Caroline has been traveling for two days, but due to heavy Bering Sea fog—first in the remote village where she sees patients, and then again in the regional hub of King Salmon—she has gotten no farther than Anchorage. She is stuck there now, having missed her connections to Seattle and Detroit, and finally to Buffalo, four times zones to the east, where she was expected yesterday. Phone calls have been made, explanations offered. Her surviving daughter Roberta, her ex-husband Charles, everyone back east says it's terrible that she can't make it. "A shame," they say sadly. But Caroline can hear the unasked question: What kind of a mother misses her own child's funeral?

After a decade in bush Alaska, cities like Anchorage are not her cup of tea. They aren't her cup of anything. Unfortunately, it is June and every flight out of the Great Land is crammed with departing tourists, nothing available until tomorrow. So she's checked into an overpriced downtown hotel, changed out of the black funeral clothes she'd intended to arrive wearing in Buffalo, and into the jeans and T-shirt she would be wearing if she were home in the village doing her job at the clinic. She's swallowed half an Ambien and a whole tizanidine but still finds herself lying on the hotel bed for an hour, eyes unwilling to close, cheek pressed to the lumpy synthetic coverlet. Beyond the headboard wall the elevator rumbles in its shaft, ratcheting its way up to the top floors of the building and then plummeting back down again, over and over until she has given up any hope of sleep. Now she sits, bleary-eyed, at a wrought iron table in the outdoor patio of a restaurant across the street from the hotel, doing the time zone math once more to the drone of stop-and-go summer traffic.

Here there is no trace of the grim weather she left behind at home. The midday solstice sun is pinned to the cloudless sky overhead. The air, thick with heated exhaust, clings to her face. After a night in a plastic chair in fog-shrouded King Salmon, and a long morning spent waiting standby in the icy chrome-and-tile Anchorage airport, the sunny patio feels like a desert oasis. It is preferable to both the forced propinquity ahead with grieving relatives in Buffalo, and the smothering attentions of the well-meaning neighbors she left behind in the village, where privacy is viewed as another weird white people's concept that no one takes seriously.

Only now does Caroline notice the hapless baby bird a dozen feet away, squatting on the top of a low stone wall that separates the patio tables from the sidewalk. It is naked, wrinkled, a featherless, bruised yellow-pink. It has stubby little wings and a neck barely thick enough to support its bald head and ghastly oversized beak. Apparently, someone has placed it on the stone cap of the wall. And there it sits, staring down at its tiny toes as though its enormous beak is too heavy to lift. It ignores the young dark-haired busboy who is trying to feed it a scrap of lunch meat.

Obviously newly hatched, the bird has fallen out of a nest. That much is clear. But what nest? Caroline throws her head back and lifts her sunglasses. She looks up at the hotel looming over the street, rows of windows upon rows and rows of windows climbing into the sunlit air. The busboy notices her and he too looks up at the glass face of the building as though a small twiggy nest might be spotted, lodged somewhere up there in all that mirrored sky, as though there will be any way to return this baby to its home—even if they can find it—as though there is something they can do.

As though there is ever anything anyone can do, Caroline thinks before she can stop herself. Okay, don't look at the bird. Don't think about it. Look at the menu. Scrambled eggs with smoked salmon. Bagel with lox. Salmon quiche. Salmon. Salmon. Salmon. It's what the tourists must want. Jesus. She might as well be back in the village.

The lunch rush is underway, the sidewalks jammed with visitors toting bags stuffed with toy puffins and polar bears. Fine-suited businessmen with briefcases, laptops, leather-bound planners hurry by. Planners, Caroline thinks. The villagers would find that hilarious and she's beginning to see why. Her daughter Sarah was to be married in October. So much for planning. She realizes she's shaking her head back and forth. She makes a conscious effort to stop.

People passing the restaurant pause to look at the tiny naked bird on the wall. A man in a Yankees hat and a blue and red track suit presses his phone to his ear and shouts, "I'm telling you, it's a baby bald eagle! Yeah, right here!" And then he walks off, still shouting into the phone. "Ugly little bitch!" Two impeccably groomed long-faced women stop to look. They grimace with such identical expressions they look like two photos of the same person, decades apart. It's a woman and her grown daughter. Caroline's throat constricts. She reaches for her water glass.

As people are seated and the crowd at the doorway to the patio thins, she realizes that the bird is not the only one sitting on the wall. Maybe five feet to one side of it, butt pressed against the stone with his back to the street and his feet planted on the brick pavers of the patio, sits an elderly man who appears to be sleeping. In spite of the warm day, he is wearing a thick Carhartt coat over a heavy cable-knit sweater. Wings of silver hair jut from the dark watch cap he wears snugged tight against the tops of his ears. A pair of aluminum crutches stands propped against the wall beside him. Sunlight bathes his face, and he smiles contentedly, paying no attention to the customers filling the restaurant patio, or to the little bird on the wall a few feet from him, or to the busboy's futile attempts to feed the thing.

Caroline's waiter appears at her side. Finally. He looks to be in his late twenties—young enough to be her son. If she had a son. But Caroline has only daughters. Two of them. No, just one now. From now on when strangers ask, she needs to remember to do the arithmetic.

The waiter introduces himself as Ari. He is dark and slender, with a long thin nose. He speaks with a vaguely European accent. He tries to tell her the specials of the day. "The salmon—"

Caroline cuts him off. "What are you going to do about that bird?" she asks.

He glances at the bird and back at her. "We are giving it meat."

"I see that," Caroline says. She gives him the look she uses on patients who persist in smoking, or in drinking and eating the things that are killing them.

"This is what they want," he says, defensively.

"What who wants?"

"This bird! It is a buzzard, I'm told." He says that in a way that implies that experts of some kind have made this determination. "They must have meat."

"A buzzard? You mean like a vulture?"

"I suppose," Ari says, watching the young busboy lay a strip of prosciutto over the little bird's beak, to no avail.

The thing does indeed look like a miniature buzzard: the grotesque beak, the featherless head, wrinkled and fleshy in a menacing buzzardly way.

Buzzards. Are there buzzards in Alaska? Caroline has seen hundreds of swans and sandhill cranes, uncountable geese and ducks and smaller birds that migrate into and out of the tundra country around the village with the seasons. But buzzards? Those she has only seen in westerns, soaring in the desert sky above a wounded cowboy, never flapping, just coasting, as though they know there is no hurry—the dead aren't going anywhere anytime soon. But it doesn't look like this baby bird is ever going to soar. Not on those short naked wings.

"It fell from a nest," Ari says, as though Caroline might not have figured that out yet. They both look up at the blue-white sky reflected in the hotel windows.

"How could it survive a fall like that?" she wants to know.

Ari shrugs. "It doesn't matter. There are dogs and cats, all sorts of dangerous animals in the city. It will be gone tonight." He leans and peers down the sidewalk, as though he expects to see a pack of slavering predators rounding the corner of the nearby gift shop. Then he straightens and says, "Would you like something from the bar?"

She looks at her watch. For the hundredth time in recent days, she adds four hours. In Buffalo they are at the graveside now. Yes, she would like something from the bar.

*   *   *

As she waits for her drink, Caroline turns her face to the sun and lets her eyelids droop, exhausted from the frustrating travel, that Ambien finally starting to kick in. It's going to be hardest on, Eric, Sarah's fiancé, she thinks. He's the one who will miss her most. That admission—that she, Caroline, Sarah's own mother, cannot even claim to be the most distressed party—is just the sort of thing that has gotten her labeled "cold" all her life. But it's true. She gave Sarah up years ago: to school and then a job on the other side of the continent, to adulthood, to a life of her own. Wasn't that the whole point of parenthood? Preparing them to leave the nest? For the past ten years they have barely talked. Why would they? What did they have to talk about? There were phone calls once or twice a year. Uncomfortable exchanges of small talk and well-wishing. But Caroline hadn't wanted to spend a lot of time with her own parents when she was in her twenties, and why would Sarah? Really, my life is not going to be all that different, she reasons. It will seem as though Sarah has moved again to yet another, even more distant time zone.

A mouthful of angry Spanish startles her. "*Pendejo!*" the young busboy barks at the little bird. He slouches back to the kitchen, defeated. The bits of lunch meat lie on the stone wall untouched, and the little bird continues to rock back and forth, but more slowly now. Caroline looks toward the bar to see what's keeping that drink.

The world has turned a bit and a shadow leans across the old man with the crutches now. He opens his eyes and looks sideways at the bird. He nods his head as though he's seen a thousand little birds just like this one. He wriggles across the top of the wall a few feet so that the sun is on him again, rearranges his crutches against his knees. He's only a yard from the bird now. When he looks up, his eyes meet Caroline's.

She looks down at her hands. A glass of vodka has appeared on the white tablecloth. A lemon twist, wetly yellow in the sunlight, lies nestled among the ice cubes. She takes a long swallow, then pulls her phone out of her purse and calls Amanda Cendillo, biologist, wildlife rehabilitator, and a friend from the old days when Caroline and everyone she knew was still trying to nurse the world back to health, one cause at a time. While Caroline doctored humans all these years, Amanda has spent her life caring for injured birds. They also talk only once or twice each year. Caroline got a card last Christmas with a photo of Amanda Cendillo wearing a Santa hat and holding a glaring, fierce-eyed owl on her arm. Amanda had written on it: "Caroline! This one reminds me of you!" Looking at the stern owl gaze, the hard-nosed, ruffled-feathered countenance, Caroline wondered if you were doomed to become the face you were born with.

"It's a baby pigeon," Amanda Cendillo says when Caroline describes the situation. "They only eat the crop milk their mothers produce for them out of chewed-up seeds. The chick has to stick its head down the mother's throat to drink it. Tell those clowns to save their cold cuts for the antipasto."

"A pigeon? Are you sure?" Caroline looks around the patio. Under a vacant table a half dozen dusty brown sparrows brawl over a crust of toast. There's not a pigeon in sight. "The beak is huge."

"The facial feathers haven't grown in around it yet," Amanda says. "I must get ten calls a year like this. Buzzards, vultures. I had a state trooper insist there was a baby condor in the parking lot of an Ace Hardware in Albany. Trust me, hon, there are plenty of buzzards who eat in restaurants, but they're wearing silk ties and suspenders. It's a fucking pigeon."

Caroline holds the phone to her ear and watches the bird tip and fall face-first into the stone tile. When it staggers back upright again, a bit of pink tongue shows at the end of its beak.

Amanda is saying, "There are millions and millions of them. We feed them to the hawks. Listen, that chick is starving. Only its mother can feed it. The ravens will tear it apart, the gulls, magpies. That's nature, Caroline. Honestly, unless you can find a pigeon that will adopt it, the kindest thing you can do is snap its neck or throw it in a river."

Caroline gets the feeling that she's the only person in the world who Amanda would say that to. There was a time she might have been proud of that. She drains her drink and clenches the lemon twist between her teeth, the acidic juice harsh on her tongue. At a nearby table a young girl listens to something on her phone, earbuds in place, head moving to the music. The obituary from the Buffalo newspaper that Caroline's ex-husband forwarded her declared that Sarah had been a follower of a band called the Tragically Hip when they toured across Canada, but recently when the band leader died of brain cancer and they broke up she became a fan of other groups Caroline had also never heard of. She vaguely remembers when she was a teen declining her own friends' suggestion to go see some famous group once. Genesis maybe? Queen? How they had teased her for having no interest in pop music. She still doesn't. She'd had to show Sarah's obituary to one of the young, plugged-in Yupik kids out in the village and ask what they knew about the Tragically Hip.

"So, besides pigeons," Amanda says, "what else is new? What do you hear from your daughters?"

Daughters? Caroline thinks. Daughter, singular now. Amanda hasn't heard about it.

"Amanda, you're breaking up! Sorry," she says, and hangs up.

She looks at her watch, adds four hours yet again. In Buffalo it's over.

She pushes her chair back. There is a popping, sizzling sound in her ears, and her head fills with foam. She thinks she's having a minor vasovagal syncope. It's the Ambien combining with the alcohol. Her knees quiver and nearly buckle. She braces herself on the back of her chair, feels the sun cooking the nape of her neck now, then straightens and breathes deeply. She'll make it. Maybe.

Out of her handbag she takes money enough to pay for the drink and lays it on the table, breathes again. Still groggy, she extracts $3 more from her wallet and clutches the bills in her fist, stands, and forces herself to take a cautious step away from the table. She should have eaten something with that drink, should have slept. Should have left for Buffalo a week ago.

The old man on the wall watches her approach. Caroline is backlit by the sun, and he has to squint up at her. She offers him the money. He slips the bills out of her fingers without ever taking his eyes off hers. "Thank you," he says. "You're nice."

This close to him she can see that he is not nearly as old as she thought at first. He's probably her age or a few years older—maybe sixty at the most. And he's not drunk or drugged-out either. His eyes are clear and alert, pupils normal for the bright noon sunlight. Hands steady. He has his crutches, and he may be homeless in this city, but sitting in the warm square of sun he doesn't look too unhappy about any of that. He looks perplexed now, though, as he examines the money she's given him. He counts it and stares at it. Then he counts it again and stares some more.

Caroline studies the bird sitting on the wall a few feet from the man. *There are millions of them.* Its wings have come unfolded and lie slumped open. Its eyes are closed now, and for a moment she thinks it's gone. But then its breast rises and falls on a big slow breath. *We feed them to the hawks.*

The man on the wall coughs theatrically. She turns to find him holding up the cash she just gave him, politely trying to get her attention. He fans out the three bills before her. One of them is a twenty. He raises his eyebrows, questioning.

Caroline looks down at the money. She feels her face swelling. The vodka seems to be trying to push its way out through the skin under her eyes. What is she supposed to do? Snatch back the twenty and say, "I'm sorry, I made a mistake? I didn't mean to give you that one? You're pathetic, but not that pathetic?"

No.

The man pushes the twenty toward her, making this as easy for her as he can. He looks away, off to one side, as if the whole thing embarrasses him. It probably does.

Caroline steps back. She hangs her purse on one shoulder, pushes her sunglasses up onto her head, and folds her arms across her chest. She says, "I'll give you $22 for your bird."

Still holding the money out before him, he turns and looks at the hatchling, then back up into Caroline's eyes to see if she's goofing with him. A smile cracks across his face. "You really like birds," he says, folding the bills into his coat pocket.

Caroline says, "I guess I do."

She stoops and reaches for it, slipping one hand under its empty belly. Its naked skin is warm from the sun, and she can feel its heart hammering away in its bony chest. Under the weight of that monstrous beak, its head lolls to one side. With her other hand she supports its head, holding its thin neck between her thumb and finger. She feels the nubby nascent feathers there and a frantic pulse beating beneath her fingertips.

Carefully she sets the bird in her handbag in a nest of damp Kleenexes. She fixes her sunglasses on her nose and looks down at it. Its head tilts up. Its beak opens hopefully, but it doesn't make a sound. Even so, she knows what it's saying.

"Come on," she says to the hatchling. Shaking off the vodka sputtering in her sinuses, she strides out of the patio. "I know where there's a big statue, down by the water. Captain Cook," she tells it. "Pigeons love that guy."

She veers into a narrow alley that leads to a little park along the shore. As she walks out of the sun and into the shadows of the buildings, she feels the chill of the sea air crawling across her uncovered arms. She can see the statue ahead, bathed in the midday sunlight, as though she's looking from within a dark tunnel. The great explorer's bronze replica peers out across the inlet named in his honor. As she assumed, pigeons loiter and fidget at his feet, pecking at the cracks in the sidewalk. Beyond him, the light fractures on the wave tips. Seabirds wheel and spin and dive, feasting on the incoming tide. Miles down the shore, at the airport, a plane departs the earth at a steep angle, a needle of steel inching heavenward with the illusory slow motion that the distance creates.

Caroline moves down the alley toward the light.

"It won't be long now," she says to the bird. "We're almost there."

Necturus Maculosus

The spring semester of seventh grade, Teddy Torameli's clothes started to shrink, his shirts becoming so tight across his chest they chafed under his arms, his pants impossible to button. Even his skin felt frankly thick and heavy and too small for him. Though he hadn't actually gotten any taller, his mother called it a "growth spurt" and took him shopping for clothes. He had also started to perspire so heavily he wondered if he might have some kind of cancer of the armpits or something.

Of course, the kids at his new school noticed. Camden Blue, one of the impossibly-grownup-looking ninth graders—the guy looked like he shaved twice a day—called him Sweaty Tits Torameli, and it got a great laugh. Tall and lean and unfairly James Franco handsome, Camden Blue was the kid in every school who knew everything you needed to know and would never figure out. Even things you didn't know about yourself. Especially those. When Camden simplified the name to Sweaty Teddy, it stuck. And because Teddy was new to the school, new to the city, new to Alaska, and wanted to know the secrets that he was sure the others kept from him, he pretended he didn't hate the name. Or Camden Blue.

Now it was June and school was out—finally, after five excruciating months—and he was alone. His mother worked six days a week at the front desk of the Comfort Inn, mobbed with tourists invading Anchorage for the short summer months. Her boyfriend,

Carl the Asshole, took up most of her free time on the weeks he was home from the oil fields.

Because his mother assured Teddy that all he needed was some exercise, he decided to walk to the sixteen-screen multiplex to see the new X-Men movie. The city still felt strange to him, the distances unclear, and the theater turned out to be much farther from their apartment than he'd realized. He trudged along the dry, unfamiliar streets, his whole body sagging under its own awful weight.

Back in Michigan, when the Asshole announced he'd gotten a job in Alaska, Teddy had balked at the thought of moving so far away from everything he knew. Carl said, "Teddy, you spend half your summers in the woods and ponds chasing frogs and shit." It was true. Each summer Teddy put together a small menagerie of toads and frogs and garter snakes displayed in well-kept terrariums on their back porch as well as an aquarium full of tadpoles and water snails, every cage neatly labeled with the genus and species of the creatures within. "Dude," the Asshole said, "Alaska is nothing *but* woods!" In the six months they'd been in Anchorage, Teddy had seen exactly one wild animal: a moose, standing in the snow in front of their apartment building chewing its cud like a stupid cow. When it started tearing branches off an ornamental ash tree, the landlord threw a snow shovel at it.

When they'd arrived in Alaska it had been deep winter, but now the summer sky was cloudless, the solstice sun high and warm, and he was sweating profusely as he walked, head down, thinking of food. Again. His stomach growled, and he glanced up to find himself in a commercial neighborhood of small, tired-looking office buildings, auto parts stores, and nail salons, all with mostly empty parking lots. There was an aging strip mall, an Asian market at one end, doors propped open. Inside, an old woman sat on a stool in front of rows of canned goods, their labels all purples and pinks and inscrutable foreign lettering. She smiled at him, and he thought about looking for a candy bar in the store, but it appeared to be entirely stocked with things he couldn't pronounce. He kept walking. Next door was a small restaurant with the word PHO on the sign and CLOSED on the door. All the other units were vacant, their doors and windows streaked and smudged, doorsteps littered with papers and plastic beverage bottles. When he came to the last storefront on the other end of the mall, he stopped.

A big aquarium sat on a metal stand in the window there, blue gravel strewn across the bottom, the water a mossy green. In the tank a fleshy, gray, lizard-like creature hung suspended in the water column, its pink gills undulating like feathers. It was a foot long with a bulbous head, tiny eyes, and a frog-like smile, four baby-fat legs with thick-fingered feet. Its smooth broad tail hung down behind it like a boat rudder. It was a fabulous gigantic salamander. A mudpuppy. Teddy's pulse surged.

Back in Michigan, he'd collected small black and yellow salamanders around the ponds between the railroad tracks, but nothing the size of this monster. And though he'd ogled pictures of mudpuppies in his *Field Guide to North American Reptiles and Amphibians* with great longing, he had never seen a live one. Their range did not extend to Alaska—Teddy knew that, of course—yet here was a beautiful specimen right before his eyes, floating so inertly he thought it might be dead. Or a fake. Maybe it was a joke of some kind? Maybe this was one of those shops that sold rubber dog turds and fake vomit. All of which would be cool. But not as cool as a real live mudpuppy.

Teddy looked around. The old woman stepped out of the Asian market, arms folded across her chest, gave him a curious look, and went back inside. There were no cars nearby, no other people in sight. He was hot and hungry, and the air-conditioned Cineplex and its prodigious snack counter beckoned to him from some unknown distance. But a live mudpuppy! He wiped the sweat from his forehead and reached for the handle of the heavy glass door.

The air inside the narrow shop was as warm as outside, and thick with the odors of moss and mold and the fetid water in the mudpuppy's aquarium. Fluorescent light tubes hummed overhead. Two rows of mostly barren shelves ran the length of the store. An empty finger-smeared glass display case sat at the far end. Behind that a brown and orange plaid curtain hung down over an opening to another room. Teddy shivered despite the humid heat.

"Hello?" he called out. Sweat trickled behind one ear. His T-shirt chafed his armpits.

The sunlight pouring in the store window turned the water in the big aquarium even greener, the mudpuppy a beautiful fleshy pink. For a moment he watched the creature's body throbbing with life beneath its taut smooth skin.

"Hello?" he said again. Nothing.

He stepped farther into the shop and saw that the few aquariums on the shelves were shiny-new and dry, the empty wire cages not yet used. Boxes of aquarium filters and lighting equipment stood stacked on the floor. A shipping label read: GREATLAND REP-TILES AND EXOTICS.

He would come back in a week or so when the store was open for business. He might even buy the mudpuppy and an aquarium to put it in. Sure. The Asshole would shit. But fuck Carl. It was his fault they were living in this strange new city where Teddy had no friends. By the time he got back from the North Slope again Teddy would have a little zoo in the apartment, his first specimen the fab-ulous mudpuppy: *Necturus Maculosus.*

True, the huge amphibian was not native to Alaska. Well, neither was Teddy.

He turned to head out the door, but the sound of shoes scuffing the floor spun him back around. A man with blocky black plastic glasses stood in the doorway to the back room holding the plaid curtain aside with one hand. He was handsome in a warm and friendly, old-fashioned way, like one of those nice dads in the old TV shows on the classic movies channel Teddy's mom liked. He wore a white long-sleeved shirt and black dress pants and looked like he should be passing the collection basket in a church somewhere. He stared at Teddy over the top of the glass counter.

"I thought you were open," Teddy said.

The man shook his head. "Not yet. But here you are. Come in."

"I already did."

"No, here." He pulled the curtain wider. "You'll want to see this. Back here."

Teddy thought the man was trying to smile. He wasn't good at it. He backed away, the nerves in his arm flabs tingling.

"Wait, look." The man pulled the curtain wider. He pointed into the room behind him. A wading pool, maybe three feet deep with white sheet metal sides and a blue vinyl liner sat on the concrete floor in the back room. A small aluminum ladder leaned against it.

"I have to go." Teddy backed away further.

The man stood unmoving, the fake smile glued to his face.

Teddy said, "I'll come back when you open!" He was almost to the door when it whooshed inward and Camden Blue walked into the shop.

"Camden!"

"Sweaty?" Camden pushed the door shut and peered at Teddy, his brow tight. "What the fuck are you doing in here?" He kept his grownup serious face locked on Teddy's. "I mean it. How long have you been here?"

"Just a couple minutes. I was leaving."

Camden glanced over at the man. "Lou?"

"Tubby just got here. Really."

Camden glared at the man. "I'm fucking serious, Lou."

"Swear to God, Cam," the man said. "Haven't laid a pinky on him."

Camden studied the man a second or two longer, then his shoulders relaxed, and he looked at Teddy again. "Okay, sure. So, what do you think of the place?" He asked that like he was trying to sell Teddy the shop. A grownup. Always a grownup.

"What do I think?" Teddy looked at the shelves of empty fish tanks and cages, at the strange man dressed for a wedding, or a funeral. "I don't know." He leaned closer to Camden and whispered, "Do you know that guy?"

Camden hesitated a second, looked like he was going to say something, but instead went to the mudpuppy's aquarium and tapped on the glass. The creature sank to the bottom, emitting a rope of air bubbles. It nestled into the blue gravel, eyes closed. "What about this beauty?" Camden asked. "You know what that is?"

"Yeah," Teddy said, unable to resist showing off for Camden. "It's a mudpuppy. Second biggest amphibian in North America." He said its Latin name.

Camden glanced back at Teddy, one eyebrow cocked. "You're full of surprises."

His attention made Teddy's ears pound.

The man said, "Camden appreciates exotics. Not many young men his age know as much about them as he does. Isn't that right, Cam?"

Camden, still bent at the aquarium, looked toward the man, clearly irritated. "I guess that's so."

The man laughed. He wasn't good at that either. He disappeared into the back room. The curtain swayed over the opening.

Teddy said, "That man. Who is he?"

Camden turned to face him. "I came in here a couple weeks ago. He was just setting up. It's going to be a cool shop. Pythons, boas, iguanas. The snakes and stuff haven't come in yet."

"But what are you doing here?" Teddy studied Camden's perfect face. For a second it looked plain and young, like any other boy's face.

"Camden," the man called out from the back room. "I'm waiting."

"Okay!" Camden's face went serious again. He stared at Teddy for another moment. In the silence, one of the fluorescent light tubes flickered and died. They both looked up, then back at each other. "Listen, Teddy . . ." Camden said.

"I think I'm going to go," Teddy said, as much as he wanted to stay and be part of whatever this was with Camden Blue. He wanted to be part of anything Camden was doing. Everyone did. But what was this?

"Wait." Camden put his hand on Teddy's arm. "You could use some money, right? I mean, who couldn't?"

"What are you talking about?"

Camden turned and locked the deadbolt on the door. "Come on." He grabbed Teddy by one elbow and steered him to the back of the store, pointing at two $20 bills sitting on the glass countertop as they walked past.

"What the heck?" Teddy said.

Camden hauled him through the curtain.

* * *

The air in the back room was even swampier than in the front of the store, and dense with the green musk of all the weedy ponds Teddy had waded into every summer he could remember, chasing frogs and turtles and water snakes. Every summer but this one.

The wading pool was filled to within inches of the top. A plastic circulating pipe drooled a steady drip into it. In the murky water a dense school of mudpuppies—there must have been a hundred of them—swam together just under the surface. The reflection of the ceiling lights shimmied on the nervous water.

"Hey, don't be afraid. Look." Camden gestured. The man who looked like someone's dad was on the other side of the pool, kneeling on a towel folded on the floor. He had rolled his white shirt-sleeves up to his elbows, folded his hands together on the metal rim. He bowed his head over them.

The room seemed to be getting warmer. Teddy felt the sweat oozing from every pore. He hated his bulging body for doing that in front of Camden Blue. "This is weird. I mean . . ."

"No, this is easy money." Camden started unbuttoning his shirt. "Do what I do."

The man mumbled something Teddy couldn't make out.

Camden kicked off his slides and stepped out of his pants.

"Shit!" Teddy whispered. "What the . . . ?"

"Nothing's going to happen." Camden went on undressing. "Listen to me."

Teddy glanced back over his shoulder at the plaid curtain covering the doorway to the front room, just a few yards away. As heavy as he'd become, he thought he was still a pretty fast runner. He could be through the curtain and out of the store in seconds. But this was Camden. Camden Blue. Teddy stayed put, his face swelling, sweating.

The man cleared his throat. "Camden?"

"In a second!" Camden stood in his black briefs now.

Teddy peered into the water. The school of mudpuppies swam past in a wide band, circling the pool, their broad tails swishing behind them, arms and legs pressed to their sides. Beneath them, the mossy blue vinyl bottom was crisscrossed with the bare footprints of someone who had walked in there.

Camden climbed out of his underpants. Teddy felt his face flush. He looked away. Then back again.

"Relax," Camden said. "We stand in the water over here. That's all he wants."

"Will our rotund friend be joining us?" the man asked.

Teddy didn't know that word, but he knew what it meant. He found himself staring at Camden's long, thin body. "I can't do this, Cam."

Camden gave him an exasperated smile. "Didn't you ever want to do things no one else does? Think about it."

Think about it? He'd spent half his life thinking about doing exactly that. Rescuing his mother from a giant anaconda. Solving impossible murders. Disarming a crazed gunman on the stage in the auditorium in front of the whole school in the middle of an assembly. Standing up to that asshole, Carl, when he talked down to Teddy and his mother. Finding his father. All the time.

Naked, Camden Blue climbed the stepladder and slid into the water up to his hips. The creatures panicked and fled from him in a mass, pushing a small wave over the far edge. The man jumped up, slapping water from his shirtfront. "Jesus Christ, Camden!" He sighed, then knelt and bowed his head once more.

"Come on," Camden said to Teddy. The mudpuppies had calmed and were swimming back toward him. "Everything's all right," he said. "Watch."

The amphibians' slick backs broke the surface as they surrounded Camden, climbing over each other to mouth his skin with their rubbery lips. The man whispered something to himself, still staring into the pool.

Teddy was certain he ought to be horrified, but then he thought about all the small zoos he'd created back home. How little black tadpoles grew into fat brown toads, and plain green ones became spotted pickerel frogs. How surprised he'd been the time an ordinary-seeming tadpole turned into a beautiful orange newt. Everything changed into something else.

This isn't all that different, he told himself. Not really.

Camden closed his eyes as the mudpuppies swarmed him beneath the water. He came up on his toes, murmuring, "Teddy, Teddy, Teddy."

The hum of the circulating pump, the muttering of the kneeling man, everything faded from Teddy's ears now except his name, his real name, coming from Camden Blue's lips without derision for the first time ever. The room grew hotter. He felt his flesh swelling in the dripping air, his clothes straining to contain him.

He looked around at the damp concrete floor, the old paint-peeling walls, the water-stained ceiling. The man kneeling. Camden naked in the water. What would his mother say? She would never know, he told himself. Besides, she was the one who had dragged him here to this place called Alaska.

Tadpoles to frogs, he told himself and peeled his T-shirt up over his head and yanked his pants down. Feeling the webbing growing between his fingers and toes, the gills sprouting under his jaw, he slid in among the creatures of the water.

"Now," the man intoned, "let us give thanks."

And that's what Teddy Torameli did, his heart swimming weightlessly at last.

Every Son Must Wonder

When my folks and I arrived in the little town on the bay on a Saturday afternoon in November, ice fog glittered in the near-dark streets as if tiny silver fish were shoaling in the frozen air. I'd never seen that before. I'd never seen winter. The digital sign at the Alaska USA Credit Union read –2°, an aberration, I would learn, for the normally temperate maritime climate. I watched my mother glance at that and then turn her eyes on our new hometown—two stoplights, one gas station, a handful of bars and pizza places, and the big regional hospital where my father was about to start his new job.

A week before, on the road from Orlando, I'd turned seventeen, and I thought I knew a few things about the world. Like my mother, for example. I thought I knew all about her. She was exactly twice my age, for instance, and twenty years younger than my father. Me, my mother, my father: seventeen, thirty-four, fifty-four. It sounded like a locker combination. She was plain and a little skinny and had small, sharp teeth, but she smiled like a young girl, a smile so genuine everyone wanted it turned their way. Men especially. At parties back home in Florida, the guys from my father's office clustered around her like bees on tupelo. It was like having a wonderfully popular big sister.

On the long drive north, we'd spent our days crammed in the Subaru, nights in the dismal motels that clung to the snowed-over prairies and mountains we crossed. And now, at the end, my mother stared out the windshield at the town, her face slack. It was like she'd left her smile by the side of the road somewhere thousands of miles behind us and had no reason to go looking for it. If she'd asked, I would've walked all the way back to Florida to find it for her.

If my father noticed the change in her, he didn't show it. He turned to me over the seatback eagerly. "This is it, Charlie. The end of the road. To go any farther than this, you need a boat or a plane."

I nodded, my eyes still on my mother. I thought she was staring at the ghostly white cone of the dead volcano on the other side of the bay, but then I realized her eyes were focused on the window glass itself, or maybe her reflection in it. Maybe my father saw that too. I was never sure how much my father saw.

"What do you think, Grace?" he asked.

"I think I need to go to confession," she said.

I guess every son must wonder what sins his mother might be capable of. I'd learned in catechism classes that even the desire to commit a sin can itself be a sin, and I tried not to think about the things my mother might want. I had desires of my own.

We drove to the town's Catholic church, St. Anthony's, a small, white clapboard building perched on the edge of a bluff overlooking the ice-choked bay, its stained-glass windows the only specks of color in the gray and white world. After confession—I'd offered up my usual litany of boring juvenile sins—we drove ten miles further up the road to a two-story house in a dense spruce forest, a house that my father, in his excitement about the new job, had purchased—furnished, but sight unseen, except for the Zillow video. We'd covered 400 wintry Alaskan miles that day on the last leg of the drive. I collapsed into a strange bed, my father's excited voice percolating through the walls of our new home, my mother's silence hovering in the cool night air.

In the morning I awoke to the sounds of them talking again, as though they'd been at it all night. My mother stood in front of the oil-fired Toyo stove in the living room wearing the ankle-length quilted down coat she'd bought online for this trip. The fabric was a shimmery silver. With the pointy hood up, she looked like a rocket ready to launch.

My father sighed, "Grace, really, check the records. This isn't normal."

"You're right," she said, staring at the dark forest outside the windows. "Nothing about this is normal."

* * *

Back in Orlando, when I first noticed that things were bad between them, my mother told my father that she needed "alone time." She rented an apartment and wouldn't tell him where. I'd heard her whispering into her phone to someone and understood that she wasn't spending her alone time entirely alone. I assumed my father had not figured that out. I didn't know whether to tell him or not, and I waited for the right time. Then, when he got the job offer in Alaska, my mother surprised us both and agreed to leave her secret apartment and make the trip with us. I told myself everything was all right again. I think my father did too. He said, "This is going to be okay, Grace. They say the polar regions are warming faster than anyplace on earth. You know, climate change! Global whatever."

"I know," she said, smiling, but not convincingly this time. "I'm sure that's true."

There was little evidence of planetary warming on the drive up. The farther north we got the shorter the days were, the colder the nights, the quieter my mother became. For the final thousand miles she hunkered down in that big coat, silent, the heater blasting her ankles, me in the back seat with my AirPods cranked up loud and the window cracked, sniffing the icy air and trying to imagine this new life we'd be starting. Somewhere in the Yukon my mother the literature major muttered, "There's a reason Dante made the worst circle of hell ice."

* * *

The weather was so awful that first Sunday in our new town that my mother considered staying home from church. For her that was like agreeing to sacrifice babies to Satan. But when zealous push came to pious shove, nothing could stop Grace Ventry from attending Mass. I wasn't sure if it was her devotion or just an attempt to find something familiar in this place.

The furnace in St. Anthony's had died during the night and the interior of the church was not much warmer than outside. In the windows the martyrs' stained-glass faces shimmered with frost. They looked like they were regretting their heroics. God the Father's white beard was fringed with ice. His son hung on the cross above the altar, half naked and freezing for our sins on top of everything else he'd suffered. Only the Holy Spirit—invisible, unknowable, and impossible to depict—escaped the punishing cold. For all anyone knew, that most mysterious member of the Trinity might have been wintering back in Florida.

There weren't a lot of warm bodies to help heat the church. Most sensible parishioners apparently interpreted the end-of-the-world cold as a sign that God wanted them to stay close to their furnace vents until He came for them. But the visiting priest, Father Brenehan, declared in a theatrical Irish brogue that this was an opportunity to demonstrate our convictions. He wore his surplice over a long wool coat and scarf, conducting the noon Mass in a cloud of devout breath. Clearly pleased, my mother followed along in her missal, eyes alive, face flushed. I could barely keep from staring at her. The three of us received Communion kneeling side by side, holding onto to the rail with our gloved hands.

After Mass Father Brenehan stood on the front steps, hatless, thick black hair writhing in the wind. He shook his flock's hands, grinning like it was a warm and pleasant Sunday afternoon someplace actually suitable for human habitation. He was handsome in that charming, unkempt way only the Irish can pull off. My mother suddenly felt like talking. If my father and I hadn't coaxed her to the car, I think she would have stood there chatting with the priest until the two of them had frozen into statues.

*　*　*

As we drove home on the narrow two-lane that wound through the forest to our subdivision, wind-driven snow twisters spun across the frosty pavement ahead of our car. My mother had gone silent again. My father started to say something to her but abruptly hit the brakes. We skidded to a stop. A Chevy work van sat parked on the shoulder of the road ahead, ladders and scaffold frames stacked on top, back doors thrown open. A man and a girl dressed in Sunday clothes struggled with the body of a large dead animal of some kind, trying to drag the bloody thing up a ramp of scaffold planks into the back of the truck.

"Holy moly! They've hit something," my father said and pulled over.

"Of course," my mother said. She nodded as though she'd known all along that we'd end up someplace like this.

It was a moose calf, only about six months old, but it must've weighed 200 pounds. Its mother, a gaunt cow moose, stood in the snow up to her lumpy knees at the edge of the forest 100 feet away, munching on willow twigs. She seemed equally uninterested in us or her dead offspring, maybe knowing she had to keep eating to get through the winter.

My father and I got out and ran to help.

In spite of the bitter cold, the girl—she looked about my age—wore just a green cloth coat over a dress and heels, the man a dark suit and a tie. The girl was tall and blond, with a zigzag scar on one cheek, a cleft in her sharp chin, and gold-green eyes gone teary in the wind. In her heels she towered over the much shorter man—her father, presumably. He had an oddly small head on a long neck, coppery hair silvering above each sideburn. His hatchet-blade face was so narrow it forced his eyes almost on top of each other. He gave us a look like he thought we were there to take that moose calf away from him.

My father said, "Let us give you a hand," and the man's fierce eyes relaxed. But once the four of us had wrestled the awkward carcass up into the van, he slammed the back doors and hurried to strap the bloodied planks up onto the ladder racks. My father yanked off one glove and held out his hand in the frigid air. "Tom Ventry," he said. "Pleased to meet you. And this is Charlie. Just moved in. Salmonberry Lane."

"Salmonberry Lane?" the girl said brightly. "We live on Salmonberry."

"Well, isn't that something?" My father continued to hold his hand out.

I continued to stare at the girl.

The man finally pulled his own glove off and shook with my father. "Jacob Dexter," he said. "That's Jane." He nodded toward the girl. "My wife."

The guy was my father's age, maybe older.

Clearly unsure what to say to that, my father asked, "Do you folks go to St. Anthony's?" As if we could've missed seeing them in the little church.

Jane smiled and shook her head. "We're Mormon."

Here was a very tall, very blond girl who was something other than Catholic. I'd attended Catholic schools all my life in Florida, gone to Catholic dances with Catholic girls—mostly short, dark, and bilingual. I prepared to be my wittiest. But inside the van a baby began to cry. Jane sighed and climbed in the passenger door.

"Much obliged for the help," her husband said curtly. He strode around to the driver's side of the van, got in, and started it. Through the rear window I saw Jane staring back over the child's seat. I was certain she was looking at me.

The van shifted into gear with a thump, and the cow moose lumbered off through the snow, snorting with irritation. My father and I stood for another moment in the piercing cold watching the huge animal until my mother tapped the horn and waved us back to the car.

At home she walked straight to the stove in the living room still wearing her coat—any warmth the Mass, the sacrament, or the dashing priest had generated in her gone now.

"They're Mormons," my father said, trying to start a conversation, "the Dexters."

My mother stared at the stove, palms out to the heat. "Well, if anyone can endure a wilderness, it'll be Mormons."

"They live down the road," I said, wondering if either of them was going to say anything about this girl being married to a man that old.

My mother looked at my father. "You should know better than to do something like this."

He said, "Grace, this is my career break. I'm not going to get another one. Not at my age. You know that." I understood that the hospital had offered him a top administration job he'd never come close to anywhere else he'd worked. "We've only been here one day," he said. "You promised you'd give the place a chance."

I looked at her, hoping she would say something reassuring.

Staring down at my father's feet, she said, "You've got blood on your cuff, Tom."

*   *   *

We'd celebrated my seventeenth birthday somewhere in the Dakotas in a restaurant called the Trough. The building was made to look like an old-timey saloon, but the parking lot was crammed with shiny Escalades and Lincoln Navigators. Wealthy ranchers or maybe oil men with thick necks and thin ties ate dinner with women in tight jeans and western shirts, lots of turquoise jewelry. My mother sat at our table bundled in her quilted coat, looking like a package of something breakable. She hadn't spoken six words all that day on the drive across the endless prairies.

My father was so happy he insisted she have one of the most expensive things on the menu, duck breast with peppercorns, her favorite. He ordered champagne because it was my birthday, and because we were almost halfway to our new home. My mother barely touched her food or her drink.

"Halfway," my father said, rubbing his palms together. "Halfway there."

When he excused himself to go to the restroom, my mother took her phone out of her purse, read a text, and pulled her lips in tight. She put it away and managed a smile for me, her eyelids heavy. "Happy birthday, Charlie," she murmured and looked around the restaurant at the glass-eyed elk and mule deer heads displayed on the walls alongside rusty farm tools and old photos of ranchers and miners and lawmen. Her eyes landed on a group of saloon girls in low-cut dresses grinning at the camera. "How young," she said. She turned back to me. "And you. Seventeen!" She set one hand on my arm. "I was your age now when you were born. You know that, right?"

She looked so serious I had to laugh. "Mom, I can do the math."

She just nodded.

I said, "Are you going to be all right?"

She looked at me for a moment and said, "Charlie, someday you'll understand that a person . . ." Then she looked up and saw my father approaching on his way back from the men's room, smiling and exchanging pleasantries with complete strangers, and she went quiet again, and I knew that we were all halfway to somewhere all right.

*　*　*

The next afternoon, after my first day in public school, the bus dropped me off at the corner where the gravel road met the paved two-lane, a half mile from our house. The temperature still hovered around zero, the air silent except for the soft squeaking of my boot soles against the frozen snow. Small black-and-white birds flitted across the road from one heavily forested side to the other, and I told myself I should learn the names of the local wildlife. I walked along thinking about my mother's use of the word "wilderness." I liked the sound of that, the idea of doing something adventurous. It was still on my mind when a big dark blue Chevy Suburban pulled alongside me, blond hair behind the wheel.

Jane lowered the window. "Charlie, right? Need a ride?"

She'd remembered my name.

I stammered, "It's a short walk."

Jane laughed. "Get in. It's freezing!"

There was a box of Skittles lying open on the dashboard, a half-full bottle of orange soda nestled in a cup holder. Jane was wearing heavy canvas work pants and a matching coat, a black knit watch cap yanked down to her ears, blond hair flaring out from under it, boots. She looked like she was about to march out into the snow and cut down a tree or check a trapline. I thought about her husband's rat-thin face, those tiny, angry eyes. But I got in.

The baby was strapped into a car seat behind us. It had a perfectly round head and a smooth wide face unlike either Jane's or her husband's. I said, "Hi, buddy."

"That's Ammon," Jane said. She put the Suburban in gear.

"Nice car." I wanted to talk about something else. "How come you went to church in the work van yesterday instead of this?"

"I forgot to plug in the block heater Saturday night. Froze. Jacob thinks it has a faulty battery."

She drove a bit further before I managed to say, "Your husband," and stalled out.

"My husband?" She looked back, behind us.

"No, I just mean . . . I just mean, he's not very friendly."

She relaxed. "Oh, yesterday? That calf? We needed to get off the road. There's a rotating list you're supposed to sign if you want to claim road meat. When a moose gets hit, the troopers call you. Jacob doesn't believe in cooperating with the police or the state."

We'd arrived at the foot of my driveway. I got out but held the door open, hesitating.

"What do you want to ask me?" she said. "Go ahead. I'm used to it."

"Your husband . . . He's older."

Her face went serious. "My mother signed for me to marry at sixteen. That's one law Jacob couldn't get around."

I stood there, still holding the door open. "You wanted to?"

"Charlie . . ." She looked at me with the kind of benevolent pity you'd offer a sadly dense family member. "My baby needed a father."

"Oh, sure," I said, like I talked to girls about such matters all the time. I closed the door and watched her drive away, a teenage girl raising a child with an old man. I, of all people, could understand that such things happen.

*   *   *

When I walked into our house I hit a wall of humid heat, the oil stove running as hot as it could go, frost ferns climbing the windowpanes. My mother was on the phone. "Yes, I'll see you soon then. Goodbye." She hung up.

"Mom," I said, "You'll see him soon? Seriously?" I wanted her to know I knew about the man in Orlando.

"It was Father Brenehan. He called to check on us new parishioners." Her eyes were bright, her lips wet.

"Oh," I said, not sure if I believed that. Not sure if I even wanted to believe it. "The priest."

She frowned. "What did you think?"

"I don't know," I lied and went to my room and stayed there until dinner, trying to do homework, though my mind kept turning to Jane Dexter, somewhere just down the road.

At dinner I noticed that my mother never mentioned that phone call—whoever it really was. I didn't say anything. Keeping my mother's secrets seemed to have become my job, and it made me feel very grown up. Anyway, my father was distracted and so wiped out by his first day at the hospital I don't think he heard anything either of us said.

That night I lay in bed listening to the icy trees scrape the roof overhangs, telling myself that I really did know a few things about the world. Just not enough. For example, why did my mother change her mind and agree to come to Alaska with us? Why did she move back in with my father and me to help pack our stuff, when every time my father was out of sight she was on her phone talking secretively? Some of the calls were long and bitter sounding. So, she had quarreled with the man in Orlando—whoever he was—but we'd just got here, and she was already talking to him again? Unless of course it really had been Father Brenehan on the phone. No, I didn't know nearly enough.

*   *   *

The next day some pipes froze and broke at the school. They dismissed us at noon. I came home to find a dented wine-colored Kia parked in our driveway. In the sweltering living room my mother was sitting on the couch with the priest, pouring tea. She wore a deep blue sweater that made her pale eyes seem brighter. She'd put on lipstick. Her cheeks were pink, her hair combed, and she looked truly warm for the first time in two weeks. She had one thin ankle crossed over the other, sitting up as straight as a spruce tree. She poured the tea and smiled at something the priest said. Handsome Father Brenehan grinned with delight, his leprechaun charm machine set on high. I said hello and told them about the early dismissal.

Father Brenehan beamed. "A day off school. Lucky lad! Charlie, isn't it? We met after Mass."

It seemed that this was a place where people remembered my name.

My mother said, "That reminds me, we saw the darnedest thing on the way home from church." She told him about the Dexters and the dead moose calf and then, lowering her voice as though Jane and her husband might be able to hear from their house down the road, she added, "They're Mormons."

"Ah, the Latter-Day Saints!" The priest winked to let me know he was goofing. "Well, you can never have too many saints, I suppose." More seriously, he said, "Good people, Mormons. Hard workers. And they help each other in time of need. I wish more of us did."

"They certainly have some funny beliefs," my mother said thoughtfully.

"Right," I scoffed. "Like ours aren't?"

"Charlie!" She gaped at me, aghast.

But the priest chuckled. "He's right, Grace. Our God is three different people at the same time? How about transubstantiation? Or the Blessed Virgin? A fifteen-year-old girl impregnated by nothing more than the words of an angel? Well, now . . ."

"That was a great miracle," my mother said, hesitantly but clearly interested in the questions he was raising.

"It was a miracle her parents believed her!" he joked.

I laughed to be polite but thought of Jane, of course, not nearly as lucky as the Virgin Mary.

My mother smiled and shook her head, still thinking about it in her charming, serious way.

I said, "So, Father, are you getting my mother to organize the ladies at church? Back in Orlando she was active in the Catholic Daughters of the Americas."

"I only wish I were going to be around long enough to do that," he said.

My mother's smile began to disassemble. "What do you mean?" she asked him.

"I'm itinerant. My time here's up. Father Silvestri will be back tonight. He's bringing Costco supplies down from Anchorage in a van we borrowed from St. Mary's. I'll drive it back to the big city tomorrow and fly out later in the night."

"Tomorrow?" she asked. "That's too bad."

I could feel the room temperature crashing. "That *is* too bad," I said, and meant it. I stood there looking at my mother's darkening face for a moment and realized she might want to talk to him alone. "Well, I've got homework," I said, and went up the stairs. I closed my bedroom door loudly, but stood in the hall, listening.

"Nice lad, Grace," Father Brenehan said.

"I can't believe you're leaving so soon."

There was a pause. "I have to go where I'm needed."

"Where you're needed." She said it flatly, but I heard the sadness in it. "I see."

Father Brenehan murmured something I couldn't make out.

"Oh," she said, "I'll have to think about that."

I slipped into my room and quietly closed the door.

* * *

There was no school again Wednesday. At breakfast my mother told my father she needed the car. "I'll drive you to work, pick you up tonight." She'd put on good clothes again and makeup. In spite of the winter morning darkness leaning against the windows, she showed the same bright spirits I'd seen the day before when the priest was there. I could see there was something on her mind. She said she was meeting with some women at the church. I wanted to ask her what she was really doing. I wanted my father to ask her.

But he just said, "Sure, take the car." He had a file folder open on the kitchen table and he didn't look up from it. Those first few days in his new job must've been murder. He stayed at the hospital late each afternoon and brought home stacks of papers, pawing through them long into the night, his computer screen glowing in the mostly dark house. "I'll call you when I get done at the office," he told her. He gathered his papers and went out to warm up the car.

I waited for my mother to tell me the truth. She glanced in the hall mirror, got into her coat, and pulled the hood up. "There're leftovers in the fridge, honey," she said without turning my way. "Be sure to eat some lunch." She pulled open the front door and stood peering into the still-dark forest. There was no wind now, the only sound the purring of the Subaru's engine. She took in a quick breath of the frigid air and started to cross the threshold.

"Mom," I said, stopping her.

Her head spun my way. With her face encircled by her hood, she looked like some kind of modern nun. "Are you going to be all right?" she asked, managing a small tentative smile.

I waited, silent. One last chance. But she said nothing more.

"I can make my own lunch," I said at last.

She said, "I know you can, Charlie," stepped out the door, and pulled it shut behind her.

*　*　*

Mid-morning the winter sun finally made an appearance in the cloudless sky, an icy white disc, as though it too had frozen. I bundled up, went out, and walked down Salmonberry Lane through a canyon of frosted spruce trees. It looked like a Christmas card. A half mile down the gravel road I came to a driveway with Jane's big Chevy Suburban parked in it. Her husband's work van was nowhere around.

The forest had been bulldozed off the Dexters' property. At the far end of the denuded lot lay a huge pile of uprooted trees, their skeletal branches densely tangled in the ice and snow, root wads pawing at the sky. There were stacks of lumber, a flat trailer loaded with cement blocks, some kind of big orange compressor or generator maybe. The house was a single-story box with gray wood siding in need of paint, mossy green shingles visible through the thin snow on the roof. A twist of acrid wood smoke curled from the chimney. Squatting in the middle of the treeless lot, the house looked very small and sad, and I tried to picture lovely Jane Dexter, or any teenage girl, raising a baby in that dreary place.

As I stood there telling myself this was none of my business and that I should go back home, the door opened. Jane appeared, wearing a lumpy yellow bathrobe. Her hair looked wet and clung to her neck. Heavy socks sagged around her ankles. The block-headed baby, Ammon, sat perched on one hip, nestled in the crook of Jane's elbow. Jane tipped her head and pressed the back of her free hand against the scar on her cheek. "I wondered if you'd visit," she said.

I looked at the baby, and the baby looked back at me like he was waiting to see what I was going to do next. That's how things happen. One thing leads to another.

* * *

When my mother didn't show up at the hospital that evening, my father, busy as always, called me and asked me to phone St. Anthony's. I spoke with the regular parish priest, Father Silvestri. He said he hadn't seen her, and asked how we were liking Alaska. I assured him we were settling in nicely. I mentioned that I had enjoyed Father Brenehan and inquired, innocently, where his new assignment had taken him. My father got a ride home from one of his staff.

Later that night he called the police, but the police said there wasn't much they could do until she'd been missing for twenty-four hours. They found our Subaru abandoned in the Safeway parking lot the next morning. The store's security cameras showed her walking away from the car, but then lost sight of her. The state troopers used a dog to track her until her trail vanished in the snow. There was no record of her departing on the commuter airline that served the town, and the Alaska Marine Highway ferry was not in port that week.

One of the investigators, a thin Black man, said, "Mr. Ventry, don't take this the wrong way, but has your wife ever done anything like this before? Because if not, then we have to start thinking foul play, and that's a whole different thing, if you see what I mean. So, is there any chance she just went off on her own?"

"No," my father said with incredible certainty. "She would never do that."

"Never," I said.

* * *

My father took the next day off work. Together we drove around looking for her, my father seeming to think she'd be out there in that bulky coat of hers wandering the snowy streets. I went along, said nothing.

In the afternoon we drove out into the hills around town, a world of gravel pits and sorry homesteads, two-track driveways strangled with naked alders, collapsing boats forever marooned in snowed-over yards. I wanted badly to tell him she wasn't coming back and how I knew that. But who wants to break that kind of news to his own father?

The days were getting shorter quickly now, and the winter sun was already descending behind the mountains across Cook Inlet when, late in the afternoon, my father pulled over into the gravel parking lot of a defunct tire shop and stopped. I looked around, wondering why we were there. When I looked back, my father had his head down, chin to his chest, mumbling something unintelligible.

"Dad?"

He looked up, seeming surprised to find me there. He sat up straighter and peered at me a moment. Then he smiled ruefully. "Charlie," he said, "how long have you known?"

I looked at my knees. "I didn't want to say anything," I said.

He put the car in gear and pulled back out onto the road and said, "Yeah. I didn't either." And we drove home through that terrible cold, both of us knowing that my mother was already someplace warm.

* * *

Friday morning my father returned to his job at the hospital and I went back to school. But first I called the police and told them the story my father had concocted: we'd heard from her; she was with relatives somewhere; it was all a misunderstanding.

Saturday I took the car and drove to St. Anthony's. The cold snap had broken by then, and God and the stained-glass saints had thawed and looked pleased once more. The interior of the church glowed in the warm colored sunlight as I waited my turn for the confessional, trying to find a way to admit what I had done. I'd been making confessions since my first Communion when I was eight years old. But this was the first time I had a truly adult sin to offer a priest. A real doozy. It had a whole commandment of its own. Plus, I had made Jane Dexter break a different one for married people.

Father Silvestri took it all very seriously. He gave me a heavy penance and made me swear I wouldn't talk to Jane again until that terrible temptation, as he called it, had disappeared from my heart and mind. I promised him on my immortal soul that I would stay away from her, and I meant it when I said it. But I was young and still wanted to believe that a person could be expected to keep a promise, or that, if things went badly, for whatever reason, he—or she—could always find a way to come back and fix the ones they'd broken.

That's what I wanted to believe.

Help

The first week of school that August, Dianne came out of the building at the end of the day and found one of her new freshmen students, Chao Saechao, standing in the emptying parking lot, clutching an armload of books. He watched the last bus disappear up the road, looking exactly as new to Anchorage, as new to America, as he was.

Earlier that day in her classroom, she'd seen enthusiasm and intelligence in his eyes, and found herself drawn to him, ready to help him if she could. She knew that her now suddenly ex-husband would accuse her of "making a project of him." Before he left her for a woman he'd met on a bicycling chat room, he'd said, "They're your students, Dianne, not your pets." But he was now halfway around the world, cycling with the new woman. So fuck him. Dianne offered the boy a ride home.

It was unusually warm for September, and she and Chao rode in the thin Anchorage traffic with the windows rolled down, the boy silent and locked away behind his wraparound shades. Dianne positioned and repositioned her own glasses on her nose, unable to think of something to talk about beyond her class and whether Chao liked it or not. In response he grunted a single syllable that she chose to interpret as positive.

Finally, Chao pointed and said, "Here," and she slowed to a stop at a corner in a dreary neighborhood called Mountain View, although there was no view of the great mountain, Denali. There were only numerous nearly identical fourplexes and sixplexes, a Quick Stop, an abandoned gas station encased in drooping chain-link fencing. A defunct Mexican restaurant squatted on one corner, weathered plywood covering the windows.

Chao opened the car door and slid out, closed it behind him.

"I'll see you in class Wednesday," she said out the open window.

He looked in but didn't respond.

"Do you understand the assignment, Chao?" She tried not to talk over-loudly or too slowly.

He said nothing, and she looked away and adjusted the rearview mirror as if it needed it, then moved it back. "Well . . . ," she said. When she turned back, Chao was gone. Just like her husband.

Halfway home she found herself on an unfamiliar street as her route detoured around a construction project where a new senior housing center was being built in an otherwise residential neighborhood. Amid the small well-kept homes, an old homesteader cabin, roof sagging, log chinking gone, was being demolished to make way for an access road to the big new geriatric facility.

At the edge of the construction site in the shade of a lilac bush sat a large dog, a malamute or husky mix of some kind. Shaggy as a grizzly, the dog had eyes so pale they looked white against the reddish fur on its face. Something about the dog made Dianne assume it was male. The size? The imperious way it lay under the lilac, basking in the late-afternoon sun like he'd put in a long day and deserved a little privacy and rest? Behind him the bulldozer smashed through an end wall of the doomed cabin and shoved it off its foundation. Collapsing timbers roared. Dust billowed into the air. The dog kept his back to all that. Near him on the sidewalk were two stainless steel dog bowls.

Across the street a woman crouched on hands and knees in her front yard deadheading end-of-summer pansies and petunias in a colorful bed along the sidewalk. Dianne shouted out the car window over the demolition racket, "Excuse me! Does that dog belong to someone?"

The woman stood, pushed a long braid of crinkly black hair back over her shoulder, and walked to the car, yellow gardening gloves clutched in one hand. Thin and dark, maybe forty years old, she eyed Dianne cautiously.

It suddenly occurred to Dianne that the woman couldn't possibly guess her intentions. In her nondescript gray sedan and her class-room sweater set—also gray—she probably looked like a person in a position of authority of some kind. Dianne laughed self-consciously. "I'm sorry. I mean, does the dog need help?"

"We've all been feeding him," the woman said, relaxing. "The neighbors and us. His owners moved away, a month now, I guess."

There was another tremendous crash and the woman looked over the top of Dianne's car. Dianne swung her head toward the sound. The cabin caved in on itself before the bulldozer's blade, lumber groaning, glass shattering. The dog looked back over his shoulder at that, and then turned away from it again.

Dianne said, "They just left the dog?" She heard how naïve that sounded. "I mean . . ." She had no idea what to say next.

"We didn't know them," the woman said. "They were renting. Never talked to anybody." She looked over at the dog. "I don't even know his name. He has a collar and tags, but he won't let anyone get close. We feed him and give him water." She paused, staring at the dog. "We used to have a dog," she said, and let that fade out.

The dog set his chin on his front paws and closed his eyes. There was another deafening crash behind him. His ears went up and then collapsed again. But his eyes remained closed.

"What's going to happen to him?" Dianne asked.

The woman shrugged. "He'll be all right until winter, but . . ." She looked up at the cloudless sky, as if the warm afternoon might suddenly give way to snow squalls. "I don't know," she said.

Dianne saw the concern in her face. "I'm Dianne," she said, and extended her hand out the window. "I teach at East High," she found herself adding, as if that explained her intrusion into this woman's life.

The woman smiled and took Dianne's hand. "Alicia. Pleased to meet you."

Dianne dug into her purse, pulled out a small notebook and a pen, wrote her name and phone number on it, and tore the page out. "Call me if there's anything I can do. I mean, for the dog. Please?"

Alicia said, "Sure." She took the paper, smiling in a bemused way that made Dianne wonder how people saw her, what they thought of her at first glance. It was a question that had not occurred to her in years, maybe decades.

She gave Alicia a smile she hoped looked convincingly sane and drove off.

* * *

The next day after work, on an impulse, Dianne drove to the construction site again, although it was out of her way. The dog was in the same place under the lilac. The log house was gone now, nothing there but the new access roadway running up to the building on the street above, a scar across the landscape. A huge truck dumped gravel onto the fresh dirt. Another waited at the curb to deposit the next load. Off to one side, a woman sat at the controls of an idling steamroller, snarled blond hair streaming out from under a pink hardhat.

Dianne glanced at the house where Alicia lived. The door was closed, no cars in the driveway. She realized she had not only come to see the dog, but on some level was hoping to talk to Alicia again. The thought made Dianne wonder how she had worked there in that small city for so many years and yet had no close friends. Had she really spent every leisure hour with her husband all that time? People said they were very close. But was that possible?

She looked at the dog again. Despite the diesel clatter of the trucks, the dog lay sleeping and apparently content in the late-summer sun, the light throbbing in the yellowing birch trees up and down the street as though the mild weather would last forever. Dianne drove off, allowing herself to believe that too.

* * *

Her student Chao, despite his apparent intelligence, immediately fell behind in her class. It pained Dianne to see the carelessness and lack of interest evident in his papers. In his face. She tried to talk to him again, but in a matter of weeks the boy had become as surly as any American-born teenager, refusing to participate in class discussions, answering direct questions in petulant monosyllables. It was maddening. She'd seen so many of the new Laotian girls flourish, doing well in school, going on to college or getting good jobs. The first-generation boys were much harder to reach.

One afternoon near the end of the month, she asked Chao to stay after class. She let the room empty and took a seat next to his desk. He stared straight ahead at the whiteboard, wouldn't turn to look at her when she spoke. He seemed much older than she remembered him from the day she'd given him a ride.

"I'm sorry to keep you late," she said. "I'll give you a ride home if you miss the bus."

He barely let her finish. "I don't take the bus no more." He continued staring ahead.

"Chao," she said, "I really would like to—"

He was already out of his chair, out the door, gone.

"Well, shit," she muttered and stared out the window at the line of yellow school buses idling in the first autumn rain, windshield wipers stuttering across smeared glass. She wondered how he was getting home. Mountain View was a long walk. And what about when winter inevitably arrived? The weather had been so mild and warm she'd almost forgotten what was coming. But the cool rain was a wakeup call. Winter would not be stopped. Would Chao be able to walk home once the snows started?

Dianne planned to talk to him again the next day, offering help after school. But he was absent. Although she taught five sections and had more than 100 other students to think about, somehow his rejection of her lingered. He didn't return to school for the rest of the week. Had her insistence on rescuing him driven him away? How would she know? It could've been anything, she told herself, glad that her husband was not around to see her trying to parse—not to mention shape—the boy's behavior.

She talked to the school counselor, Barry Kalapu, an imposing muscular man who, not being locked in a classroom all day, knew as much as anyone about what was going on among the students. She asked him to check up on Chao, thinking that the counselor might extract some answers from the boy. "I'm hoping that you—being a man—you know, might get through to him."

"Don't get your hopes up," Barry said. "I'm Samoan. He's Laotian. You ever see the Asian kids hanging with the Pacific Islanders around here?"

"Oh," Dianne said. "I hadn't thought of that."

"Chao's running with a bad bunch," Barry told her. "That much I know."

"A gang?"

Barry shook his head. "Sort of. Maybe more like punks with similar interests."

"Interests?" Dianne said, hopes rising. "What kind of interests? Maybe I—"

Barry snorted.

She felt her face flush.

"Dianne," he said. "I'm sorry. Really. I didn't mean to laugh." He grimaced and ran one enormous hand through his silky black hair. "Let's just say, you don't want to know about their interests."

It took a few seconds for that to sink in, and once again Dianne was embarrassed, but this time also a little angry with Barry for assuming, correctly, that she had little real knowledge of what her students were up to out there in the world outside the school.

"You know," he said, "some of the Laotian mothers told me that they moved up here from L.A. to get away from the gangs down there." He sighed. "The thing is, their sons *are* the gangs."

Dianne thanked him and left, wondering if she'd always been this out of touch. Twenty-five years of teaching. Jesus. Maybe it was time to retire.

*   *   *

As the last days of the month further shortened and cooled, shoals of clouds moved in from Prince William Sound, delivering mixed rain and sleet on winds howling down off the mountains. Wet brown leaves clogged gutters and clung to windshields, and the streets flooded with muddy runoff. But Dianne was buried now with papers and exams to grade, classes to plan. She had little time to think about Chao. Or much of anything else.

On the first of October she came out of the school an hour past quitting time and was startled to find the nearly empty parking lot covered with an inch of soggy snow. Huge conglomerate flakes cartwheeled around her. She stepped over slush puddles, wishing she had brought her boots. She thought of Chao, wherever he was, out there in the weather.

He had not returned to school. Neither the principal's office nor Barry Kalapu had been able to locate him. Someone from the school district had also attempted to contact the boy. No luck. It wasn't clear if his own family knew where he was staying. A social worker was involved but had no good information. Dianne had asked some of the Laotian girls about him, but they merely rolled their eyes and shrugged, really only interested in boys—mostly the industrious Filipino boys—who were going to make something of themselves. Who could blame them?

She drove to Mountain View through the falling snow. Parking at the corner where she'd dropped Chao, she realized she didn't know which building he lived in. She could've gotten the address from Barry or the main office, but now it was too late to call. She hadn't thought of it, hadn't thought any of this through very well, she realized.

All the fourplexes looked the same. Tan or gray wooden siding, cheap white plastic window frames, scratched-up metal doors with peepholes. Dianne got out of the car and walked through the wet snow to the closest door and knocked.

A skinny, very pale young woman answered the door. She had a skinny pale baby on her hip. "What?"

"Hello," Dianne said, "I'm looking for the Saechao family."

"Say Chow? I don't know any Say Chow person."

"They're Laotian," Dianne said, immediately wondering what good that might do. "Asian?" she tried.

She opened her mouth to say something more, but a man's voice boomed from somewhere inside. "Who's at the door, Sylvie? Not those Witnesses, is it?"

The woman turned. "Somebody looking for some Chinese folks."

The man's voice again. "Tell 'em there's a bunch of Koreans both sides of that green duplex on the corner. Maybe they know something."

The woman turned back to Dianne, repositioning the baby on her hip. She shrugged, indicating that was all Dianne was going to get, and closed the door.

For the first time in days, Dianne thought of the dog.

*　*　*

The access road to the senior facility was paved now, the property landscaped. Chemically green hydroseeding radiated through the new snow covering the contoured grounds. The lilac bush was gone. But the dog was there, sitting upright, regally, wearing a small crown of white.

Dianne parked at the curb and turned the motor off. She rolled her window down to keep it from fogging and watched the way the snow accumulated on the dog's reddish fur, amazed he didn't bother to shake it off. Was he that resigned to the indignities heaped on him of late? Abandoned. Home destroyed. How much was one animal to take?

She sat a little while longer, wet snowflakes wafting in the open window.

If she could get close enough, she could talk to the dog. She could calm him and hold him by the collar and walk him across the street to the woman named Alicia. Then Alicia would have a dog again, and the dog would have a home.

Dianne looked up and down the street. There was no one around. She put two fingers to the corners of her mouth and whistled, something she hadn't done in years. They'd had two dogs once, she and her husband: Welsh corgis, funny stubby-legged things, long ago when they'd first moved to Anchorage. The whistle came out shriller and louder than she'd expected. It was one of the few things even he had to admit she did very well.

At the sound, the dog's head jerked her way. He peered at her with interest, as though he might know her. Then he stood and shook the snow off his coat.

She stepped out of the car and waited a moment, holding the door open. The dog watched her, his tail low and rigid. Soggy snowflakes smeared her glasses, but she didn't reach for them. She pulled her leather gloves off and threw them on the seat and took a step toward him. "Hi," she said. "Hi, buddy."

The dog looked through her.

She approached, talking all the way, heart speeding, hoping to see that tail wag. Nothing. But he didn't back away either. And then she was only a few feet from him, the dog apparently open to her overture of friendship. This was going to work. Talking calmly, she reached out one hand to let him smell it.

The dog stood its ground, tail still straight out behind it. He had such a sweet face. Those pale eyes—up this close she could see they were blue—searching Dianne's face for something. Something Dianne was sure she could provide. It really was going to work. She took another step.

The dog lunged.

"Jesus fucking Christ!" she yelped, yanking her hand back, a dull throb pulsing in the tips of the two fingers he'd nipped. "Get back!" she screamed. She staggered backwards, squeezing the aching fingers with her other hand, kicking slush at him. She kicked again, harder. "Back! Back!"

Her fingers were seeping blood now, but still she could see that the dog's attack had just been a warning. He crouched, looking like he was about to really go for her this time. For her face? Her throat?

"Go!" Dianne screamed, scrambling away faster now. "Get! Get!" She stamped her foot and kicked at him again, slipping, almost falling in the wet street as she backed away. "Get!" she screamed. "Go!"

Now the dog shrank back, cowed. And that was the worst thing of all. You'd think that winning an argument would make you feel good. But she'd won so few. What did she know? His cringing posture stabbed her.

"Wait," she said to him. But he had turned away, skulking across the white expanse where his home had once stood until he disappeared around the corner of the new senior center. "Oh, dog," Dianne sobbed. "Goddamn you."

She remained standing at the edge of the road, squeezing her bleeding fingers in her other hand, sniffling. It was not even 6:00 but the streetlamps were already glowing against the gloaming sky. The long nights were coming, her first winter alone in Alaska. "You fucker," she muttered—not at all sure who she meant.

The snow fell harder. Her fingers throbbed, and her shoes were soaked, but she stood there in the gutter a while longer watching the blood slow and thicken on her wounded fingertips. Wondering about Chao Saechao walking home in this miserable weather. Wondering what was going to happen to that dog. Wondering where her husband—her ex-husband—was just then. Bicycling somewhere warm and sunny and exotic with the new woman, that much she knew. But where? Thailand? Vietnam? Bali? She couldn't recall. Maybe that was a good sign. Did it mean that she didn't need him any longer? A kind of freedom? Or did it mean that she didn't need anyone, might *never* need anyone again? Was she going to become one of those women? Independent? Or just simply alone?

One thing she knew for sure. She needed to go home and work on her lesson plans. It was only October, and the first of the standardized tests was coming up already. By spring the teachers and students alike would be sick of them. And Dianne would be weary of the onerous paperwork. Though, really, she thought, without the constant tests, how would you know if you were ever getting through to anyone? How would you know if you were helping?

She was about to walk back to the car and drive home through the darkening neighborhoods, but instead she crossed the street and knocked on Alicia's door.

The door opened, and Alicia stood in the warm entryway, a glass of wine in one hand. "Dianne? What on earth?" she began, then raised her eyes to look over Dianne's shoulder. Dianne turned that way. At the corner, a man on a fat-tire bicycle raced by, splashing through the wet snow, his rear tire hurling a steady stream of slush up onto his back. Oblivious to that, he looked up at the two women, and in the light of the streetlamp Dianne could see the reckless joy on his face. She shuddered.

Alicia turned back to her. "You're cold. What happened to you?"

Dianne still looking out at the street, held her bloody fingers out to her but said nothing.

"And you're bleeding!" Alicia said. "Do you need help?"

Dianne watched the man on the bike disappear into the falling darkness. "Yes, help," she said. "I think so. I think I do."

Time on the Water

I

After the company downsized him out the door, after his divorce, after the heart stent went in and a section of his colon came out, Alan resolved to spend more time on the water. He knew that this was just a way of dealing with the fact that Gwen got the big house in Anchorage and he got the cabin on the river 200 hundred miles south of town, but he was determined to chalk up some small entry in the win column. When the papers were finalized, he filled the pickup with fishing gear and boxes of Costco groceries, then rolled down the aluminum mini-storage door in front of everything else he owned in the world. Would he come back for them? He had a feeling that this was the kind of thing you don't come back from.

He'd dodged the COVID bullet and thought he was doing all right. And then just about everything else inside him went to shit. Jesus.

He drove south onto the Kenai Peninsula, craving a cigarette so badly he found himself checking the ashtray for butts, smoking being at the top of the long list of things now forbidden. Snotty raindrops smeared the windshield and peppered the grassy muskrat ponds along the road. It was August, the wet season starting, although May, June, and July had all been rainy too. The way things had been going for him, he had little hope that September and October would be any different.

The way things had been going. What were the chances your wife would leave you for someone with the same name? Hers, not his. Well, since it had been Gwen's decision to separate—and since Gwen II had the cash to help her buy him out of what pitiful equity they had in the house—he got an admittedly fair deal in the split, everyone reasonable and speaking in indoor voices as they'd taught their kids. And in truth, he hoped the two Gwens would be happy together. Still, on some level, he regretted not having any lunatic-ex-wife stories to bolster his injured-party status.

*   *   *

At Anchor Point he turned onto the gravel road to the bridge over the river. The plywood-skirted trailers, the sagging shacks, roofs draped with blue vinyl tarps, the dead cars and trucks in every other yard, all gave the place an air of despair he'd almost forgotten over the winter. But the rain had quit thirty miles north at Clam Gulch and the sky was now a sunny blue expanse, the spruce trees along the narrow road fragrant in the late-evening air, the drying gravel coughing up dust clouds behind him in his rearview. This might be all right.

The river looked clear and fishable when he crossed the old steel trestle bridge at the highway turnoff—new graffiti scrawled across one big I-beam read, EAT ME, BEAT ME, MAKE ME WRITE THAT CHECK—and the silver salmon should be coming in from the sea in numbers soon. It might be good. He could use a little good luck.

He hit the brakes 100 feet before his cabin, gravel pillowing beneath his tires. A low, deep-red muscle car sat nosed into the apron of his driveway, two shadowy figures sitting in the front seat. He tapped his horn. The night was quiet for a moment, except for the fidgety warble of a nuthatch chiseling the dusty air. Then the strange car started up with a shuddering blast of a song his daughter used to torment him with, a hip-hop version of some old '60's hippie anthem. He couldn't remember the name. The car backed out and came his way, hard against the alder bushes on that side of the road, the thundering bass line vibrating its windows. He pulled over to give it room.

It was a Pontiac Firebird, the aging candy-apple paint pocked with gravel dings, black plastic trim duct-taped in places. Alan couldn't say what year. He'd never been a motorhead, had always driven Ford pickups. They would run forever. Which was more than he could say about himself now that his doctor had finally used the "C" word.

The Firebird drew even with him, the naggingly familiar melody muted a bit. The driver-side window rolled down and a thin-faced blonde in her late teens—a bit younger than his daughter—stared up at him from behind the steering wheel. She had keen eyes and a taut, strong jaw. She spoke confidently. "Sorry, mister." It sounded more like a prepared statement than an apology.

"Sure," he said, a little bemused by the girl's poise. "No problem."

The passenger, a boy about the same age, leaned across the girl's lap to look up at Alan with eyes so slitty they may have been closed. His hair, black and straight, fell across his shoulders. When he spoke, a dark smudge of first-growth mustache moved with his upper lip. "Yeah, man. Sorry," he said, with none of the girl's maturity.

The girl gave Alan one final frank appraisal, hit the gas, and they were gone.

If he weren't at least twenty-five years older than her—not to mention an overweight, balding collection of infirmities—he would have sworn she'd been flirting.

The name of the song flashed into his head. "In-A-Gadda-Da-Vida," the melody buried now under the huffing, puffing gangsta groove. Why would anyone remake that? Because the original hadn't been bad enough? It was like striving to synthetize athlete's foot. The hip-hop artist was one of his daughter's favorites. Maybe that Fiddy guy? Or possibly Diddly? One of those names you had to let people call you because you'd lost a bet.

*   *   *

Alan hadn't been to the cabin since the end of the steelhead season the autumn before, the intervening ten months now a fog of job applications, divorce papers, and unpleasant talks with his daughter. Then there came the really unpleasant talks—with his oncologist. Well, at least those wiped out the need to look for a new career.

He could imagine some human resources interviewer asking him where he saw himself in five years. That might be fun to answer. He was trying hard to view that as a silver lining of sorts.

He carried an armful of gear up the wooden stairs onto the deck. A pile of porcupine scat—tiny extruded logs of compressed wood fibers—lay heaped on the threshold as though the UPS man had stacked them there. Alan pushed the door inward and watched a single spiderweb strand sag between the doorknob and the wood-stove pipe on the other side of the living room. It looked like it would be just him and one hell of a broad-jumping arachnid. He'd take what company he could get.

As he turned to shut the door, the red Firebird rolled past the end of the driveway again, going the other way. No music this time, just the low rumble of the muscle-bound engine and the rhythmic ticking of a sticky valve or two. He watched the girl's profile as the car passed. Chin up, eyes straight ahead, driving like an adult. Looked like kids in Anchor Point grew up quickly.

But what were they doing cruising up and down the subdivision road? He tried to empathize. That was what his oncology counselor advised. "Think about other people's problems too, Alan, not just your own. Find the humanity in their lives. In them. It'll keep you human."

Oh, he was all too human. The always-fluttering heart. His aware-ness of the cancerous cells somewhere inside him right now flip-ping a tiny malignant coin, deciding whether to go full-bore deadly or toy with him a while longer. Going to bed alone and waking up alone a little stiffer and slower every day. He was pretty sure those weren't the kinds of things animals lost sleep over.

Okay, empathy. It must be rough living on a dirt road in low-rent Alaska. Moose in the front yard, bears in the back. The nearest town fifteen miles away, and that nothing but a cluster of tourist shops, bait shops, and coffee shops. The nearest mall 200 miles north. And then there were the endless life-sucking winters. There should be a reality show called *Tragically Bored Teenagers of the North*. It wasn't exactly divorce, financial ruin, and cancer. But still, it probably felt that way to them. Poor bastards.

There. He felt better. Empathy. That was Alan, Mr. Empathy.

*   *   *

He made what he hoped was a suitably healthy dinner—a lamb chop and a salad—and opened a can of Mountain Dew, as much as he wanted a glass of wine. Amid the various dietary restrictions heaped on him in the past year, he was supposed to be cutting back on the alcohol now too. He wasn't sure why he was bothering to attempt any of those healthy restraints, except that it might allow him to momentarily believe he could somehow survive all of this. Still craving a smoke, he ate ravenously instead.

To avoid thinking about those things, he would fish the early tide the next morning and then drive into the town and set up a post office box, start notifying everyone of the change in address. Everyone. That meant his insurance company, his cell phone company, the doctors he owed money, and the half dozen fly-fishing magazines he subscribed to. His daughter wouldn't need his address. She communicated digitally. She did everything digitally, as far as he could tell. The physical world was of very little interest to her.

He ate the lamb chop, worrying about money. The pittance from the house and the small parachute the company gave him before shoving him out of the corporate door were nearly gone. He wouldn't live long enough for Social Security. He ate the salad, worrying about worse things than money.

The evening dragged on in the lingering summer daylight. He rigged his fly rod and checked the tide book—the low tide tomorrow would start turning around at 7:34 a.m. He set his alarm and climbed into bed, picturing the silver salmon milling in the salt chuck waiting to ride the morning flood upriver. He kept the bedroom window open to listen to the resident horned owls, and he was almost asleep when he heard gravel crunching under tires, the tick-tocking of bad valves.

Empathy, Alan. Empathy.

*   *   *

In the morning he slept right through the alarm and awoke two hours after the low ebb, too late to fish. He cooked ham and scrambled eggs and loitered his way through a pot of coffee. On the way into town, he stopped at the local gas station, Atkins's Garage. Their unleaded was 5 cents a gallon cheaper than gas at the stations in nearby Homer, where the town imposed a thick layer of summer taxes on anything that might tempt a tourist to crack open a wallet.

Atkins's Garage had no automated credit card pumps, and as Alan stood fourth in line at the cash register, Visa card in hand, it occurred to him that he was the only person paying with plastic, and that all the other customers were Anchor Point locals. The shaky young woman in front of him gripped a 20 in one skinny fist and kept clawing her unnaturally black hair back behind her ears with her free hand, twisting and pulling it like she was trying to yank it out. In front of her a heavy guy about Alan's age, likewise holding a bill between two thick fingers, rocked from foot to foot, slow-dancing to music only he could hear.

At the register, an old lady—a septuagenarian at the very least and five feet tall at most—took a pile of small bills and a roll of quarters from a cadaverous, ghost-white woman wearing what appeared to be a flannel nightgown and flip-flops, rings on every finger, both thumbs, and half her toes. On the wall overhead, a sign apologized for not accepting checks "Of Any Kind!"

How far could you get on $20 worth of gas at today's prices? Maybe these people just never left this place.

When Alan paid with the Visa card, the old lady at the register smiled and said, "Thank you and welcome to Anchor Point" with sardonic formality. "Where're you visiting from?"

"I just moved here, actually."

"Here? Really?" she asked, incredulous. "Retiring? You look a little young for that."

"What makes you think I'm retiring?"

"God knows there aren't any jobs here."

They both laughed.

She said, "Well, I guess I'll be seeing a lot of you then."

Alan left, feeling oddly elated by the unexpected friendliness. Out front, the walking dead gal wearing the nightgown was getting into a bashed-up Subaru, a cigarette dangling from her lips. Alan veered out of his path and walked close enough to inhale a lungful of secondary smoke. It was all he could do not to go back into the station and buy a pack of something.

He was halfway back to his truck when the red Firebird rolled into the parking lot, the girl from last night at the wheel again, her passenger seat empty this time. She honked and waved, smiling like a cheerleader on mood elevators. He looked back over his shoulder to see who she was aiming all that sunshine at. There was nothing behind him but the gas station. Alan waved back, hesitantly. But she'd already swerved back out onto the highway again. It almost seemed that she'd detoured through the gas pumps to greet him.

Weird.

* * *

The evening tide would be low at 7:45. Planning to stay out fishing late, Alan made a tuna sandwich around 6:00 and took it and a glass of Mountain Dew out to the small metal table and chairs on the front porch. His rod and tackle and waders were already sitting at the top of the stairs. He'd taken one bite of the sandwich when the Firebird pulled into the driveway and parked behind his truck. The girl got out. Alone again.

She waved with more glee club enthusiasm. More friendliness, he told himself, though she was clearly selling something. Handbag over one shoulder, she strode up the stairs onto the porch. He asked her to sit, offered her half his sandwich. She was quick to accept. Her name was Angela. He fetched her a plate for the sandwich, some pickles, a can of Mountain Dew, a clean glass. He sat back down.

She told him that the boy in the car, Dace, was her brother.

"His name's Dace?" he said, oddly pleased to hear he was her brother. "Like the fish?"

"There's a fish called a dace?" she asked through a mouthful of tuna. She reached for a pickle slice. "I didn't know that."

Alan let her eat for moment in silence. Then he couldn't wait any longer. "So, what can I do for you, Angela?"

She reached into her purse, pulled out a pint of Wild Turkey, poured three fingers into her glass, tipped the can of Mountain Dew into it, and tasted the concoction. She took another bite of her sandwich, wiped a smear of mayo off the corner of her mouth. "I want you to help me rob the gas station."

Alan laughed. "That's funny."

She wasn't smiling now. Beneath her pert, girl-next-door nose her lips were as level as the horizon. She waved the whiskey bottle at him and raised her eyebrows quizzically.

He felt a sudden need for a drink. He took the bottle, poured. "Jesus. You're serious?" It was the single most interesting idea he'd heard in months. And the most hopeful.

She locked her clear green eyes on his. "You in?"

"Do I look like a criminal?"

"No. That's why, silly. You look like every other older kind of fat fly fisherman."

"Thank you," he said. "Thank you for pointing that out." He took a swallow of his much-improved Mountain Dew.

"I just mean that Old Lady Atkins has known me since I was born. But you? Shit. Every morning there's like a hundred guys who look just like you standing in the river wearing rubber pants and throwing hooks at fish. Even if you didn't wear a mask, that half-blind old cow couldn't pick you out of a lineup in a thousand years."

Alan ran his fingers through his beard, trying to figure out why he wasn't just laughing the kid off the porch. He could leave her and go fishing. How many happy hours had he spent doing that in his life? Lots. Alone, of course. "How old are you?" he asked.

"Seventeen, two weeks ago."

"And why are you robbing somebody you've known all your life?"

"Because pot's legal now, and that's going to drive prices down for the stuff I've been selling since I was twelve." She paused to take another bite of her sandwich. "I want to make one last buy and sell it off before the prices start crashing. I've got money saved, but I need more to buy a bigger-than-usual shipment."

"And what's in this for me?" he asked, still half thinking it was all a gag of some kind.

"I'll give you a share of the cash from the register." Her face shifted from all-business to something more seductive. "Unless you want to roll over your share and invest it in the weed I'm going to buy."

"If you want investors, why aren't you just asking me to invest my own money in this?"

She looked like she was going to laugh. "Your money? You're driving a ten-year-old F-150, not even an extended cab, the cheapest piece of crap that Ford makes. You're eating tuna sandwiches for supper." Angela's face went back to its dead-serious mode. "How much would you like to invest, sir?" she said, and chuckled.

She looked like she might get up and leave. He really didn't want that to happen. "All right, let's say we're going all Bonnie and Clyde. Why not just rob a bank and get real money?"

"Because Atkins's Garage doesn't have an alarm system, functioning security cameras, or armed guards. And last time I checked, robbing a gas station was not a federal crime."

"Well, you do have a point there."

Now she smiled. "Okay, good. Here's the plan . . ."

"Wait a minute! I didn't say I was going along with this."

"Sure you did." She smiled. "You said it with your eyes."

Alan glanced at his watch. If he wanted to fish the tide change, it was time to head to the river. But, he told himself, there was no harm in hearing her out. He took another long swallow of his drink. "I'm listening."

As he had surmised, many of Atkins's customers were hard-luck locals, very few of whom were ever going to qualify for a credit card, no matter how lax the banks got. The local economy was either cash or barter, and Atkins's was not going to barter for gas, Angela explained. "They take in around a thousand a day in cash. More, some days."

She said that Mrs. Atkins only went to the bank once a week, on Wednesdays, letting all the cash accumulate in a safe in her office until then. Each Tuesday night she counted it, put it in a canvas bag, and made out the deposit slip for the next morning's trip to the bigger town on the bay.

"How do you know all this?" he asked.

"Oh, I worked there for years when I was a kid."

"When you were a kid." The whiskey and the low evening sun were creating a fuzziness in his head. Maybe his meds were contributing too.

"I have copies of the keys to every door in the building," she said.

"Then why don't you just sneak in there one night after the old lady is gone and take all that loot yourself?"

"It's in the safe at night. I'd have to blow the thing up or drag it out of there and pound on it like a monkey with a coconut." She paused, looking at him like she wasn't sure he was capable of understanding. "I'm trying to keep it quick and simple. You see?"

"How do you know I'm not going to just call the cops right now?"

She shrugged. "You didn't call the cops last night when me and Dace were doing God knows what in your driveway."

"What were you two doing, by the way?"

She frowned and looked at him like she hoped he wasn't foolish enough to think she was going to tell him.

"Fine, but what makes you think I'm going to commit a felony for you?"

She chuckled. "I know an adventurous soul when I see one."

She pushed back her chair and stood. "Thanks for the snack. I'm going to make a few deliveries. You go fishing and think about it. If you could use a couple thousand and a little excitement in your life, let me know. Here's my digits. Call if you're in." She set a scrap of paper on the table and went down the stairs to the driveway.

He called out to her as she reached for the Firebird's door handle. "You wouldn't have a cigarette, would you?"

She shook her head and slid into her car. "That shit will kill you."

Alan watched the Firebird disappear behind the wall of alders lining the driveway. He drained the last of his drink and studied the piece of paper with her phone number on it. He wondered if he did indeed look like a guy with an adventurous soul.

He went into the cabin and poured himself another Mountain Dew with a heavy slosh of Kirkland bourbon, still half planning to fish the low tide. But every sip of the drink reminded him of the girl named Angela, a phenomenon he replicated several times until he fell asleep sitting up on the couch.

*   *   *

An hour after low tide he awoke to Angela pounding on the front door. It was getting dark, the owls calling now.

"Looks like you forgot to go fishing." She pointed to his gear, still sitting on the porch, high and dry. "I'll fill you in on the details."

"I thought I was supposed to call you if I was interested."

She scoffed and pushed past him. "You're interested."

Alan pointed to the kitchen table. She took a seat. He poured her a drink. Did it really matter if you were giving alcohol to an underage girl if you were plotting a felony with her anyhow?

Angela was all business again. "Tomorrow night Old Lady Atkins will be in there after closing, counting the money. You go in through the back door, grab the bag from her. Then you take her cell phone, yank out the landline, lock her in her office, and take off. We'll meet back here."

Alan felt a cloud forming in his brain, either the alcohol at work or molecules of simple common sense trying to coalesce. Maybe both. "I'm taking all the risk, girlie," he said. "I'm not sure I'm liking that."

"Come on, what's the old lady going to do, hit you with her purse? She's like a hundred years old, for Pete's sake."

"I could use the money," he said, although he knew well enough that this had nothing to do with money.

Angela smiled. "There you go." She reached into her purse and pulled out a rubber Hillary Clinton mask and handed it to him.

"Do you have a pantsuit in my size?" he joked.

"No. But would you like a gun?" She reached into her purse again.

"God, no! No guns! Jesus."

"I'm kidding." She showed him the inside of her purse. "You won't need a gun." She stood and pounded down the rest of her drink. "I'm going to roll. I'll see you right here tomorrow night around 9:00. We'll celebrate."

And with that she was gone.

Alan's heart felt all fluttery, his brain fogging like it wasn't getting enough oxygen, a feeling his doctor said to expect more often now. The question was, for how much longer? He poured himself another drink. Piss on the doctors. If he'd had cigarettes, he would've chain-smoked them until he passed out.

*   *   *

Tuesday he woke with a minor hangover and plenty of time to fish the morning tide, but somehow burned up several hours doing dishes and sweeping ten months' worth of dust and cobwebs out of the cabin. Lunch also turned into a tedious ordeal. By midafternoon he'd fallen asleep from nervous exhaustion and didn't wake up until his phone rang. He flew off the couch as though electrocuted, but it was only Gwen the Original wanting to know what to do with some old fishing tackle she'd found in a corner of the garage.

Gwen. Her voice diced him. He had no idea what to say.

"Alan, are you still there?" Gwen said. "The fishing tackle. What do you want me to do with it?"

"Throw it out," he yelped and hung up, heart flipping around now like a beached salmon.

Trying to calm himself, he turned on the radio and mostly ignored *All Things Considered* while binge-eating a whole box of Wheat Thins. Then he slept again, fitfully, until it was nearly time to go to Atkins's. There had been no word from Angela all day. Somehow he resisted the urge to call her.

*   *   *

A little before 8:00, dusk announced itself in the long cottonwood shadows reaching out over the road. Alan parked across the highway from Atkins's and waited until the neon OPEN sign went dark. He drove across the road, parked behind the gas station, and tugged on the Hillary mask. All thoughts of the two Gwens, his cancer, the medical bills, the river and the fish gone now, he got out and slid Angela's key into the back-door lock. As he crept past the candy and motor oil displays, past the coffee counter and empty cash register, past the locked cigarette cabinet, he could hear the rhythmic mumbling of the old lady in her office, counting.

She sat bent over her desk, peeling $10 bills off a stack, an old gooseneck lamp throwing hard yellow light across the bank deposit bag and the bundles of cash around it. "Eight hundred and ten, twenty, thirty, forty..."

He stepped close behind her chair. "I'll take that!" His words sounded loud and rubbery inside the mask. He kept one hand in his jacket pocket.

He'd expected her to startle, but she just paused, reached for a pad and a stubby yellow pencil, and calmly wrote down the last number she'd intoned. She set the stack of bills down and swiveled her chair around to face him. In the stark lamp light, she really did look a hundred. Her cloudy eyes, wildly magnified by her glasses, peered up at him from a contour map of fleshy mountains. "You make me lose count, I'm going to get all itchy," she said, decades of cigarettes resonant in her voice.

"Just put it in the bag and hand it over." Alan was sweating profusely inside the mask. "Come on!" he barked, surprised and a little pleased with the shrill voice that came out.

The old lady looked at the hand in his pocket and sighed. "You didn't think to bring a gun, did you?" She lifted the canvas bag off the desktop and pulled a huge silver pistol out from under it. Pointing the weapon up at his face with two heavily spotted hands, she said, "I sure hope not."

"Shit!" He threw his hands up. His heart relocated itself somewhere near his Adam's apple and went on fluttering there. "No, ma'am."

"Good," she said. "For God's sake, take that silly mask off. There's some in these parts would shoot you on sight, on the chance that it really was that woman."

Heart spinning, he pulled off the Hillary mask, held it up dangling from his still-raised hands, unable to take his eyes off the black mouth of the enormous gun.

She squinted up at him. "Hey, you're the fella retiring here, right?" He nodded.

She set the pistol down on her desk, picked up a pack of Marlboros, lit one with a Bic. When she'd taken a deep drag, she said, "So, where'd you meet my granddaughter?"

"What?" He lowered his hands. "Angela?"

"Where did she find you? You're older than most."

"Older than most what?" he asked, brain sluggish.

The old lady laughed. "That girl." She shook her head. "She's a caution." She inhaled deeply again, set the cigarette in a butt-heaped ashtray, and picked up the stack of bills she'd been counting. "Listen, son, I got to get this cash added up. Let yourself out the way you came in and lock up, would you? Give the key back to Angela when you see her. And like I said yesterday, welcome to Anchor Point."

"Wait," Alan said. "You've been robbed like this before?"

She smiled at him. "I'm not being robbed."

"You know what I mean. You're telling me she's sent guys in to try this before?"

"It's a just a little game her and me play sometimes," the old lady said. "She finds an ordinary man—not one of the halfwit thugs and tweakers around here—a regular upstanding citizen. And she bets me she can talk them into committing a serious crime. You know, somebody like you."

"Like me?"

"She's such a cynical girl. I hate to see that in young kids today."

"She sends someone in to rob you, and you chase them off with that gun?"

Mrs. Atkins shook her head. "Not usually. That's new. Usually I give them the money, and Angela brings it back the next day, minus what she has to give the guy. But I'm tired of fussing with all that. So I bought the gun just recently. Makes it simpler. She doesn't know about the weapon. I'll still give her credit for talking you into it."

"Just my luck." Alan slumped onto a tall wooden stool next to her desk. "Suppose I could have one of your cigarettes?"

She smiled and shook one halfway out for him. "It breaks my heart. It really does. The cynicism. But I have hope. Sometimes a month goes by without her finding a candidate."

"A game?" He lit the cigarette and sucked in the smoke. It was his first since his diagnosis. He felt his whole body thanking him for it. "What'll she win for pulling me in?"

"A share of this week's money." She shrugged. "I'd give it to her anyway, of course. She's my favorite. Her brother's a moron and mean. Bad combination. Just like their mother. Angela's saving her winnings, along with her weed money, for college. She knows I'm going to pay for that too, but she likes the challenge. Good girl, really. Ambitious." She gave Alan a look of grandmotherly pride. "Now, I really do have to get back to work here, uh . . . ?"

"Alan." Woozy, he stood. "I guess I better go." It came out sounding as pathetic as he felt.

"Don't look so grim, Alan," she said, concerned now. "Life is good. Tomorrow you'll go fishing, catch some nice salmon. And someday when you're old, you'll tell your grandchildren about the two crazy women you once met here. They'll laugh and think you're making it up!"

"When I'm old," Alan said with a sigh so loud the old lady winced.

"Hey, come on, son. I don't mean to run you off. Stay a bit if you want."

The pity on her face stabbed him like a call from his radiologist.

She said, "I've got a bottle of something around her somewheres."

He shook his head no, then thought about it. He really didn't have anywhere to go, anyone to meet. He could do anything he wanted now with the time he had left. Somehow, fishing didn't seem like a major attraction anymore. She was right about one thing, though: life was good. That was the whole problem.

"Sure you don't want a drink, hon?" She waved a bottle at him.

He said, "Thanks, Mrs. Atkins, but I don't think so," leaned across her desk, and picked up her cigarettes and the pistol.

II

He drove.

He drove, chain-smoking Mrs. Atkins's Marlboros. That's what you do after a stickup. You jump in your truck and drive away from the scene of the crime with a cigarette in the corner of your mouth. Even an admittedly ineffectual robber of gas stations like Alan had seen enough movies to know that much.

He drove up the two-lane highway out of Anchor Point, heading north, of course. South went nowhere: a dozen miles to the town of Homer, and then a few more miles of residential sprawl and a handful of small businesses east of town. Beyond that there were only a few hardscrabble homesteads, a couple Russian villages at the desolate head of the bay, and then the Harding Ice Field, as big as a small country, and the absolute end of the road. Period. So, with night deepening across the pavement ahead of him and the rising moon full, or nearly full, still showing in the gap between the horizon and the ceiling of heavy clouds, he drove north with the enormous pistol on the seat nestled against his thigh.

There were few cars on the road at that hour, one or two pickups towing skiffs heading south toward the fishing grounds, a boxy brown UPS truck, a gill-netter's stake-bed piled with nets and floats and brailer bags. Just north of Anchor Point a bashed-up junker that may have once been a Toyota Corolla lurched out in front of him from a side road and crawled along at less than half the speed limit, oily gray smoke pluming from under the one intact rear fender. Alan finally passed the thing to get out of its exhaust cloud. The driver, a wizened skinny old guy in a conical short-brimmed plumber's cap, clung to the steering wheel, squinting through the spiderweb cracks in his windshield. Alan used to dread getting that old. Used to. Now, he'd be willing to take his chances with a dotage in total decrepitude if it meant just a few more years.

He drove, glancing into his mirrors repeatedly, expecting flashing lights, sirens ripping the night air behind him. There was nothing in the mirrors but the gathering darkness. The farther north he went the thinner the traffic became. Weedy fields and dense spruce forests flew by, a few small rivers running under narrow bridges, the moon floating on them like a bright yellow bobber. He drove through the little crossroad towns of Stariski, Ninilchik, Clam Gulch, and Kasilof, each one a jumble of shabby buildings huddled under weak lamp lights. Each with a tiny post office, charter fishing companies, and Thai or pizza places. In their parking lots heavy sport boats perched on trailers awaiting the morning fishing, downriggers clamped to their transoms. A store featured a tall sign with three words stacked on top of each other: Coffee. Cigarettes. Ammo. He glanced down at the pistol on the seat and kept driving, lit another Marlboro.

In an hour it was fully dark, the moon lost now above the cloud bank as the highway bent eastward toward Soldotna. That was the direction a serious criminal escaping from a serious crime would go, of course. Not that it would do any criminal a lot of good. It was another 150 highway miles to Anchorage, and then 400 more spanning the vast empty tundra and forests of the interior of the state before eventually connecting Alaska with the rest of the continent at the Yukon border. One cop with a nail strip could stop anyone stupid enough to try that route. There was simply no good way to drive away from a crime here. There was no good way to drive away from anything. All of which begged the question of whether anyone was even looking for Alan. Had anyone found Mrs. Atkins yet? Had Angela gotten tired of waiting for Alan at their scheduled 9:00 rendezvous and gone to the gas station to check on him? With no answer to those questions, he decided to simply drive until the next thing happened.

Not in the mood for Soldotna—a stultifying hodge-podge of strip malls, car dealers, and fast-food joints—he veered off onto Kalifornsky Beach Road and drove toward the town of Kenai. Beyond that there was only the little oilfield town of Nikiski, another absolute dead end like Homer, and not as scenic. Then what? He'd know when he saw it.

Kalifornsky Beach Road was even emptier than the highway. Not a vehicle in sight for the first five miles, nothing to slow him down. No obstacles in his path, he thought, enjoying the fussy, somewhat formal sound of that phrase.

He had spent much of the day trying to muster the nerve to rob the gas station. Then the actual attempt and the conversation with Mrs. Atkins had produced a dizzying tension that fueled his drive this far. Now he found himself drifting across the center line and jerked the wheel hard right, careening onto the shoulder. Gravel exploded against the undercarriage, sounding like it was hitting his eardrums. Jolted awake, he drove on, adrenaline coursing through him. Temporarily. In another minute he was nearly asleep at the wheel again, his mind blissfully empty of everything once more.

He let himself drift now. How much better it might be to careen off into a tree, or even veer off onto the next side road heading toward the bluff over Cook Inlet and just keep going, shooting out into the thin air until he hit the surface of the water 100 feet below. How much better that sounded than the protracted death by cancer or his failing heart that seemed to be in store for him if something more interesting didn't happen first.

He was still entertaining those dreamy thoughts when someone or something walked out onto the road in the beam of his headlights. A cluster of legs. He jumped on the brakes with both feet, pulse surging. "Jesus!"

The odor of scorched rubber filled his nose as the truck shimmied to a stop. Ten feet from his front bumper, a cow moose and her twin calves loitered in the road on their long legs, blankly staring at Alan's truck like it was the most interesting thing they'd seen all day. Wide awake now, heart twisting, Alan attempted to get his breathing back to normal. This is why moose are more dangerous than bears. Because they are so fucking stupid! This was why there are big signs along every highway, tallying the number killed on the road each year. Four hundred? Five hundred? Eight hundred? Unbelievable.

He rolled his window down and lit another of Mrs. Atkins's cigarettes, wondering how long the moose family intended to stand there. When headlights appeared in the distance—he could see it was a big vehicle approaching at the speed that every commercial truck driver is going to try on a straight and empty rural road—he said, "Time to go, Mama Moose." The moose blinked at him. "Go!" he shouted and hit his horn.

The cow moose bolted across the right shoulder of the road and on into the darkness of the trees on that side. One calf darted after her, but its twin remained standing directly in front of Alan's truck. Dumbstruck at all the commotion suddenly filling its very new world, it looked for its mother and then back over its shoulder at the oncoming vehicle barreling toward it, then back at Alan.

Alan honked his horn again, turned his four-way flashers on, and hit his bright lights. He banged on his door with one arm out the window, yelling, "Get out of here!" But the calf just blinked at him with bulging, uncomprehending eyes. The truck—a big flatbed stacked with heavy fish totes—was almost on them now, the driver laying on his air horn and flashing his powerful brights, but not slowing. The young moose gave Alan a quizzical look as though asking what Alan thought it should do. It took a step toward the oncoming lane. "Not that way!" Alan screamed as the approaching truck arrived, and the calf walked out into the blur of its oncoming lights.

Alan looked in his mirror and watched the red taillights fading into the mists, the sound of the big truck's horn dopplering off behind him. The odor of diesel exhaust and fish lingered in the cooling air. Had he heard a thump? The sound of the calf smashing against the truck's grille? He leaned out the window, listening intently to the silence of the empty night. After a moment he was about to drive on when he heard a sound from the darkness of the ditch on his left. A soft cry? He listened harder. The wind whispered through the forest on the bluff above Cook Inlet. Waves murmured on the beach below. Nothing more.

Then a moan cut the night. Alan shut the engine, stepped down out of the truck, and lit the flashlight on his cell phone. He leaned back into the vehicle and took the pistol off the seat. Nervously looking back over his shoulder, he walked over to the ditch. Of all the stupid things he'd done in the past two days, getting between a moose cow and her calf was shaping up to take first place. The old lady's handgun was a monster, but it wouldn't stop a charging moose.

The calf lay at the bottom of the ditch in a heap of brown hair. It peered up into Alan's flashlight beam writhing hopelessly, unable to rise. One leg jutted out at a terrible angle. It didn't look hurt otherwise, although Alan understood that a broken leg was a death sentence for a wild animal. Again, he looked back over his shoulder and up at the road where his headlights and pulsing red flashers threw the only light in an otherwise black world. Still no sign of the mother moose. He cocked the hammer of the pistol back and stepped closer to the softly bleating calf.

With the blast from the big pistol ringing in his ears, he climbed out of the ditch, heart fluttering. The idea of aimlessly driving north suddenly had little appeal. Again he wondered if anyone was looking for him. The only crimes he had in fact committed—aside from the petty theft of old Mrs. Atkins's cigarettes and handgun—were unlawful trespass, possession of an unlicensed firearm, and of course the half-assed attempted robbery. Not much by Anchor Point standards. He had to face the fact that he might not be a hunted man, as disappointing as that was. He got back in the truck, turned off the four-way flashers, and started the engine. Making a U-turn, he headed back south.

When his lights fell across the stairs to his porch, he was surprised to find himself parking in his driveway, having no memory of the drive home from Kalifornsky Beach Road. He half expected to find Angela sitting there at the little metal porch table, incensed that he'd failed to get the money. But there was only the neighborhood porcupine ambling away across the porch and down into the alders. Exhausted, and enervated by his anticlimactic and completely unneeded getaway flight, not to mention the numbing effect that executing the little moose had on him, he staggered upstairs and fell, still fully dressed, onto his bed.

* * *

In a strangely dry mist, Alan wandered through a forest listening to owls hooting to each other across the tops of unfamiliar trees—a lovely dream until persistent hammering on the cabin door yanked him out of it. Crawling back into consciousness, he strained to hang onto the pleasant, foggy state a little longer, but the continued pounding drove the last wisps of it away. He glanced at the clock: 1:43 a.m. The clouds had lifted, and the moon was back in full force. Moonglow washed across Mrs. Atkins's nickel-plated revolver where it lay on the nightstand. He could see the primers on the remaining brass cartridges in the cylinder. The knocking got louder.

This was it. The police. Finally. Probably the state troopers—they had a station right there in Anchor Point, less than 100 yards up the highway from Atkins's Garage, the scene of the crime. Such as it was. This was definitely it.

But it wasn't.

He realized that the insistent knocking was all wrong, and his fantasies of a dramatic confrontation began to fade like his lost dream. The knocking was thinner, lighter than the sound he imagined the knuckles of a full-grown cop would produce, and certainly too slight for the gorillas the state troopers hired. With little enthusiasm he kicked off the covers and swung his feet to the wood plank floor. He'd fallen asleep in his clothes, even his shoes, on. Sitting hunched over his knees, he peered out the window. Angela's Firebird sat in the driveway, glowing a rather demonic red in the wavery moonlight.

She shrieked, "Alan! My grandmother wants her goddamn gun back!"

He smiled. He'd never heard anyone say anything like that before.

A shadow flitted past his window, one of the owls heading for quieter environs. No dream this time.

He slid the window wider. "Angela, hush! You're disturbing the wildlife. I'll be right down." He took the pistol off the nightstand and snugged it into the waistband of his pants behind his back and pulled his sweater down over it. It felt like something an actual fugitive from justice would do.

He went downstairs and unlocked the door. Angela shoved in, crashing the door back against the wall, where Alan's still unused fly rod hung straddling three wooden pegs. Alan reached to keep the rod from bouncing off the wall. "Come in, Angela," he said, calmly. "You're up late."

"What the hell, Alan? What the hell?"

He said, "What's on your mind?"

Angela glared. "My mind? Where have you been all night? I came here at 9:00 like we said." She waved her cell phone at him as if confirming Alan's unexplained absence. "You didn't show up, I went to the gas station and found my grandmother locked in her office, sitting on her money, complaining about her missing cigarettes. And her gun."

"The gun," Alan said. "That was a surprise."

Angel calmed a bit. "I wouldn't have sent you in there if I knew the crazy old bat had a gun. Honest."

"I drove around for a while." He walked to the kitchen table, shook a cigarette out of the Marlboro pack, and lit it. He thought about telling her about the moose calf, but the memory of it made his throat thick. "Sit. I'll make some tea."

"You drove around? I don't even want to know. Just give me the gun."

"Yeah, the gun," he said. "I don't have it anymore." He went to the stove and put the tea kettle on. He pulled a small flowered teapot out of the cupboard, looking at its yellow and blue flowers. Back when he and Gwen first built the cabin near the river, she had bought the teapot at an arts fair in Homer to offset the manly fishing-shack ambience. "Have a cup of mushroom tea," he said to Angela now. "It's organic."

"Alan!" she said. "What do you mean you don't have the gun anymore? Where is the goddamn gun?"

"Your grandmother shouldn't be waving that thing around. Somebody is going to get killed. Probably her." Alan fussed with the tea. "This is called chaga. It's supposed to be an antioxidant. Made from tree fungus or something. Ever had it?"

"Fungus." Angela collapsed into a chair, head in her hands, elbows on the tabletop. "My grandmother doesn't need the gun, Alan," she said. "*I* need that gun. And I need it right now. What have you done with it?"

He felt the weight of the big pistol lodged in the waistband of his pants. The day he and Angela had shared his tuna sandwich and drank Mountain Dew highballs on his porch making their preposterous plans for the robbery, she'd seemed like a kid trying to look grown up. Now she looked more like a grown woman trying to pass herself off as a teenager. It didn't seem like a situation a gun would improve. Then again, he couldn't think of many that a gun would.

"I threw it into the Kasilof River when I drove over the bridge."

Angela sighed. "Please, Alan, stop screwing around? I really need that gun!"

"I like your grandmother," he said. "She told me about the game you two play." He fixed the tea and put the teapot and two cups on the table. Strange, mossy-smelling steam rose from the spout of the teapot. He sat across from her again. "Come on, Angela. Tell me what's going on. What do you think you need a gun for?"

Angela studied him. Her cocky teenage poise returned for a moment. "Man, you turned out to be a real pain in the ass. You know that?"

"You're not the first woman to say that." He poured two cups of tea. "You're telling me this isn't about your grandmother?"

Angela shook her head tiredly. She thought for another moment, apparently deciding whether to trust Alan with whatever was going on. Finally she said, "The guy in the car with me the other night in your driveway wasn't my brother."

"Not Dace?" Alan was still tickled by that name. One of the first trout flies he'd learned to tie as a young boy was called the Black Nosed Dace.

"No, not Dace. It was a guy named Chico."

"Is that his first name or last?"

"I don't know! Chico something, I think."

"Chico something? Okay. And how do you know this guy?"

Angela blew on her tea. She wrinkled her nose and didn't drink. "I bought some dope from him."

"So what? According to your granny, you've been doing that for years."

She shook her head. "Not weed."

"Not weed?" he said. "What, then?"

"Fentanyl."

"Oh, man . . . What are you doing screwing around with that stuff?" He had been enjoying this conversation until that point.

"There's just no profit in weed anymore," she said. "When people can get it at the cannabis stores, what do they need me for?"

Alan had to wonder if legalizing pot might have the unintended consequence of reducing its usage. Without the rather thrilling feeling of defying the law that he used to love when he was young, legalized pot smoking seemed as mundane as everything else in ordinary life. Shit, they put the stuff in gummies now. Chewing on sticky little gumdrops had none of the heady outlaw vibe you got from palming a smoldering joint, imagining every cop on the street is looking at you. That was the best part of it.

"Alan, are you listening to me?" Angela said.

"Yeah, sure. What's the problem? Your grandmother will give you money."

"For college she will. Or even for weed. But fentanyl? She's not going to help me with that."

"Well, I can see why. Christ, Angela." Trying to take all this in, Alan drank a sip of tea. It was possibly the worst thing he'd ever tasted. He set the cup down. It was too late for antioxidants anyhow. "This guy, Chico whatever, you do realize the Feds are probably onto him, right? Following him? Tapping his phone? Which means they already know about you."

"That's not what my problem is right now."

Incredulous, Allan scoffed. "Oh, you have bigger problems than the DEA coming for you? Great. Can't wait to hear this."

Angela tasted her tea and made a face. "Jesus, this tastes like the underside of a log. Where's your whiskey?"

He pointed to a cupboard. "Help yourself."

She stood with her cup. Alan held his cup up to her, the muddy aftertaste from the tea clinging to the roof of his mouth, the fungus probably already growing there. "Better dump mine too. Bring the bottle." His heart was acting up, but he couldn't tell if it was more than the usual fluttering he was destined to live with. Maybe a drink would help.

Angela emptied their teacups into the sink and pulled the bottle of bourbon down out of the cupboard. She splashed some into her cup and then into his. She was seventeen years old. Was his daughter doing shit like this when she was seventeen? Thankfully, he had no idea.

"Angela, what have you gotten yourself into?"

She sat back down opposite him. "I owe Chico money." She drank from her cup and grimaced at the burn from the bourbon. "I have to give him 10,000, and I only have about 5."

"Or what?"

She looked up at him. "What do you mean?"

"What happens if you don't pay him?"

"Are you crazy? He's a drug dealer. He knows people in Mexico. What do you think is going to happen? He's going to do things to me, things I don't want to get done to me. Not by him, not by anybody." She sniffed. "That's why I'm here. I can't go home. He's looking for me."

Something was wrong with the story. "Nah, I saw that twerp the other night in your car. He looks like he's about fifteen years old."

She came halfway out of her chair. "Well, he's not! He just looks young. He's twenty-two. And he's dangerous!"

Her eyes were wide with what he knew was supposed to look like terror. But he had seen real terror only hours before in the moose calf's eyes, rolling in the beam of his flashlight as Alan pressed the muzzle of the big pistol against its head. That was real. This? This might be just teenage emoting. Then again, what was the harm in finding out? He was up in the middle of the night with a gun in the back of his pants, drinking bourbon with a crazy seventeen-year-old girl. Meeting Chico sounded like the next thing an outlaw would do.

"All right, all right," he said. "Take it easy. I'll help you. Tell him to come over here."

"You don't have $5,000 to give him." She sank back into her chair, eyes blurry.

Alan wanted to believe those were real tears. At the same time, what difference did it make? If this whole fentanyl story was another fake on Angela's part, then she was in no real danger, and neither was he. And if it was the real deal? Well, he'd been hoping for something important to happen. This could be it.

"I can pull that much money together," he said. "I'd have to go to the bank in the morning."

She looked up, eyes not so wet now. "You'd do that for me?"

"Hey, if you don't pay me back, I can always rob a gas station, right?"

Angela laughed. She wiped her nose. "So you really think you can get the money tomorrow?"

"Sure, but let's call this Chico character and invite him over and tell him about it. You know, get his take on it. Make sure it's okay with him."

"No, no, no. Don't bring him here."

"Come on. I'll reason with him." This was the best he'd felt since the gas station.

"This is a bad idea, Alan. Chico's not somebody you want to mess with. He looks soft, but he's not. I'll go with you to the bank tomorrow." She tried to smile but didn't manage it.

"Yeah, yeah, yeah," Alan said, waving that off. "Just dial him and give me the phone. I'll do the talking. I want to meet the person who's getting my money."

"You're insane," Angela muttered, but she punched a number on her phone. "It's me," she said. "I can get you the money. Someone wants to talk to you." She handed Alan the phone.

"Yeah, this is Alan," he said. "I'm a friend of Angela's. You and I met the other night in my driveway."

The kid talked rapidly.

Alan said, "That's right, the old guy in the Ford truck. Yeah, Angela's here now. Come on over. Yeah, right now, sure. It's past my bedtime but I'll try to stay awake till you get here."

He hung up before Chico said anything more.

Angela held her forehead in the palm of one hand and drank her bourbon with the other. "You don't know what you're doing, Alan. This is not good."

Maybe not, Alan thought, but it's something.

*　*　*

He had never been a brave person, never a hero of any kind. Never served in the military. Never been in a bar fight. He hadn't been in a fistfight since third grade, when Jeff Benuti beat him up on the playground of Cartsville Elementary because Jeff thought Alan was flirting with his girlfriend Katherine Diaz, a gorgeous Irish/Mexican red-haired beauty. Thinking about this now made Alan wonder what Katherine Diaz was doing these days. Was she still back in Cartsville? Was there a way to look her up on the internet? Facebook?

"What are you thinking about?" Angela asked him as they waited for Chico to arrive, still at the table with their teacups of bourbon.

"Why?" he said, not wanting to admit that after a lifetime of myriad fears—heights, drowning, large dogs, small dogs—he was more than a little baffled by his current equanimity. A supposedly dangerous drug dealer was coming to settle a score, and he felt as tranquil as a Zen master.

Angela peered at him. "Because Chico is coming to probably kill me, and probably you, and you were smiling."

"I was thinking about Kathy Diaz," Alan said. "A girl I liked in third grade."

"Third grade." She closed her eyes, locked her jaw. "You're daydreaming about third grade girls?" She opened her eyes and frowned quizzically. "What happened to you last night since the gas station? You're different. What did you do?"

Should he tell her that her grandmother's words about life being good were echoing in his head when he stood over that little moose calf in the ditch and blew its brains out?

He opened his mouth to say something, but just then they heard gravel crunching on the driveway.

Angela stiffened and tossed back the rest of her drink like an old alky. "Aw, jeez," she muttered. She wiped her lips with her fingertips. "It wasn't supposed to be like this."

Alan sensed that he should ask her what that meant. Then a car door slammed.

With Angela's eyes locked on the front door, Alan eased Mrs. Atkins's pistol out from behind his back and held it on his lap under the table—again, because it seemed like the kind of thing a real desperado would do in a situation like this. He searched his feelings and found nothing resembling fear or even mild concern. His fluttering heart felt normal to him now. He wasn't sure if that was a good thing. Then again, once you got used to the reality of your own impending demise, what was there to fear?

Footsteps thudded across the porch. The front door flew open, crashing against the wall behind it again. This time Alan's fly rod clattered to the floor. The kid Alan had seen two nights before in the front seat of Angela's car hesitated a second on the threshold as though remembering what he needed to say. "What the fuck, Angela?" he screamed. "What in the fucking fuck?"

He had a high voice and sounded like a bad actor delivering bad lines. He looked even younger than Alan remembered from their brief exchange in the driveway. Barely five feet tall and thin as a child, he was dressed in a denim jacket and jeans like a tiny cowboy. He wobbled unsteadily on the threshold of the doorway in pointy-toed boots, feet apart, hands on his hips, elbows flared. His hair was black and limp and draped to his shoulders, his mustache equally soft and fine. His eyes were the same sleepy slits he'd trained on Alan from the front seat of Angela's Firebird.

"Hello Chico," Alan said. "Come in. Have a drink."

"Who the fuck do you think you are, asshole?" Again, a script of some kind, and not a great one.

"I told you on the phone. I'm a friend of Angela's."

"Well, then say goodbye to your friend." Chico strode into the cabin, pulling a small black pistol out of his jacket pocket. "Because I'm going to put this bitch in the ground." He brought the muzzle of the pistol level with Angela's head.

She closed her eyes and whimpered, "No, please. He can get the money for you."

Chico glanced at Alan but then noticed the flowered teapot on the tabletop. He leaned a little to look closer, like he'd never seen one before. He straightened. "I don't see any money," he said. "All I see is a lying bitch and her old fat friend having a fucking tea party." He tightened his grip on his gun and tensed. "See you in hell, bitch."

"Chico, wait," Alan said quietly. "You don't want to do that."

The kid swung the pistol Alan's way. "You rather be the first one dead, dipshit?"

"Not really," he said. Raising Mrs. Atkins's heavy pistol, he held it just above the teapot and pulled the trigger for the second time that night.

Over the blast from the enormous pistol, he heard Angela wail. "No, Alan, don't!"

The boy lurched back six feet, the impact of the heavy slug driving him backwards, causing him to moonwalk like a wounded Michael Jackson toward the open door. He raised the pathetically small pistol, pointing it directly at Alan once again.

"No!" Angela screamed again. But again too late.

Alan's second shot launched Chico out the door and across the porch, arms cartwheeling. He disappeared off the top step.

"Alan!" Angela crashed out of her chair.

"What?" His ears were ringing, his eyes watering from the nostril-stinging odor of gunpowder. That brought the moose calf back to his mind. Unlike Chico, the calf merely shuddered and went still when the bullet entered its brain, its neck going limp, its head settling peacefully against its shoulder.

Angela was still screaming at him. "You fool!"

"He was going to shoot you!"

"Dace!" Angela howled, running out the door onto the porch. "Dace!"

"Dace?" Alan set the pistol down on the table, walked outside, and stood next to Angela at the top of the porch stairs, heart twitchy again. "What?"

"You killed him," Angela said. She'd gone calm, trembling and clearly aghast. "Alan, you killed Dace," she muttered. "You killed him."

"You mean Chico," Alan said, trying to get his heart calmed, his brain straight. "He was going to shoot us!" His mind swam. "I thought his name was Chico."

"You, you!" Angela spun on him now, wild again, slapping him madly. "There is no Chico! You old fool. You stupid, stupid old fool! There never was! That's my brother Dace!"

Alan put his hands up to ward off the blows, the realization of what had happened swelling in his brain, something else swelling in his chest. Angela gave up and staggered down the stairs. She knelt over her brother's crumpled body. The boy's legs were bent under him, arms sprawled across the gravel. He still clutched the small black pistol in one hand. In the moonlight it looked like a toy.

"Look what you've done," she moaned, shoulders sagging. "Dace, Dace, Dace."

Alan slumped and sat on the top step, heart ratcheting up to a frantic pace he'd never felt before, legs numb, arms tingling. The porch began to spin. The spruce trees along the driveway danced. An owl hooted once and went silent.

Had he taken his pills when he got home from driving to Kenai earlier? He couldn't remember. He remembered the moose, and he vaguely remembered the owl dream, and he remembered Angela pounding on his door to wake him. But everything else was dim and misty now.

Through the fog in his brain he heard Angela cry, "You were supposed to give us the money, Alan!" She sobbed. "That was the plan!"

But Alan was gone. Gone down to the mouth of the river across from the old volcanoes with his fly rod, down to the surf line where the clear outgoing freshwater blurred into the silty brine. With the huge late summer tides, there would be several hours between the low turnaround and the high slack water of the flood. Plenty of time to spot the silvery salmon bulling up the estuary shallows on their way home. Plenty of time to finally fish.

III

The sirens brought him out of his stupor. He could hear them screaming in from either Anchor Point or Homer. Maybe both. Ambulances? Local cops? State troopers possibly.

He pulled himself up from the step he'd collapsed onto, his heart racing, but not a lot worse than normal now, his head clearing. Angela was still hunched over her brother's body, silent. In the moonlight they looked like some kind of religious statue. How long had they sat there? Should he say something to her? What do you say to a person whose brother you just killed?

The sirens sounded much closer. He needed to move.

Alan hurried across the porch and into the cabin. The pistol was lying beside the teapot on the table where he'd set it after shooting Dace. Lifting it, he considered trying to escape in his truck, but Angela's Firebird was blocking his driveway. Her purse was on the floor next to her chair. He bent, lifted it onto the table, and fished her keys out.

Angela didn't look up from her brother as Alan came down the stairs and stepped around her. She didn't look up when he got into her car and slammed the door shut. She didn't look up when the Firebird's huge engine turned over with a muscular roar and the hip-hop she was listening to on the radio blared out into the night. She didn't look up.

And Alan didn't look down. Not all the way down. Not down to the ground where the dead boy lay. He didn't want to look at that. He'd rushed away from the dead moose calf in the ditch, and he was rushing away from this too.

He got the car radio under control and was backing down the driveway when an explosion of blue and red lights erupted behind him with a whooping alarm blast. A Homer Volunteer Emergency Services ambulance turned up his driveway, every light on it flashing, blocking him in. Alan turned off the ignition.

He slid the big pistol into the waistband of his pants again and tugged his sweater down over it. The EMTs grunted some kind of hello to him and hurried past Angela's car and Alan's truck and crouched over the inert body of Dace. Angela stood now, sobbing into her hands, watching the medics attempt to save her brother. She still hadn't registered Alan's attempt to take her car, and she didn't look up to see him standing there next to it now.

Alan strode around the back of the Firebird and pushed into a gap in the alders. The alders closed in on him immediately, and with their dense leaves shading out the moonlight, the interior of the thicket was dark, and he stumbled every step of the way. Eventually, he fought his way out of the densely tangled alders and into the more open spruce forest. There was enough light seeping through to see his way around the shadowy low branches of the big trees.

He plunged into a ravine heading downhill toward the river. The ravine was thick with brutal undergrowth. Thorny devil's club bushes tore at his hands, and jagged spruce branches clawed his face as he crashed down to the rivulet stream at the bottom. Panting hard, he stopped, feeling the cold trickle soaking his shoes, wishing he'd brought water to drink.

He rubbed at a welt rising on the side of his neck and hoped it was from a simple tree branch and not anything that left stinging toxins in his skin. What was he doing? Why was he running? The kid broke into his house and pointed a gun at him. Alaska is a stand-your-ground state. He would never be charged with the shooting—not if he'd stayed and told his side of the story. But what was his story exactly? That he got duped twice by the same teenage girl? That he shot her brother in the middle of what Alan believed was a drug deal using a gun he'd stolen from the girl's grandmother? It was so preposterous Alan almost laughed. Until he thought about it. He'd killed a young boy. What happened to the idea that life is good? Everything wants to live, right? Even teenage punks and baby moose.

Well, he couldn't change any of that now.

Sweating, he pressed on, following the little stream through the thick underbrush until he could see brighter moonlight up ahead where the forest opened out onto the soggy bottomland along the river. There the moonlight was bright and clear on the tall grasses and elderberry thickets, the low berry patches, and the broad leaves of still more ferocious devil's club bushes. He pressed on. If he could get across the river and up the other side of the valley, he would be on the highway. Even in the middle of the night, a trucker or motorist might stop for a clean-shaven, late-middle-aged man in decent clothes. As long as he kept the gun hidden.

He followed the small rivulet that would lead him to the river, his shoes soaked now, pants wet up to his thighs. Plunging into a stand of tall stiff-stalked plants, he realized too late that he was thrashing through pushki. Their thick tubular stems were six or seven feet high this late in the season, the white flower clusters on each top going to papery seeds. But their irritating toxins were still active, and Alan could already feel the tingling on his hands and face, and he knew that—if he lived to see the morning sun—his skin would erupt with painful blisters from the ultraviolet rays.

He climbed up onto a rocky knoll and looked over the field of pushki to see how much farther it was to the river. In the moonlight the flower heads glowed and the whole river valley seemed to be covered in a ghostly silver shroud. From there he could see the other side of the valley a half mile away, and he watched the flashing lights of a police or emergency vehicle of some kind racing along the highway, sirens wailing, horn blatting faintly at that distance. Then, behind him, he heard more sirens shrieking in from the secondary road to the cabin. He rethought his plan to hitchhike.

If he still wanted a vehicle, there would be cars and trucks at the campground two miles downstream where the road crossed the river on the old iron bridge. People would be asleep in their tents at this hour. But he already knew there was no way to drive out of trouble on a peninsula with only one road on it. And this time there was no question of whether the police were looking for him or not. He pushed on toward the cottonwood trees lining the riverbanks. Over the years he'd come this way many times fishing for steelhead, but that was later in the fall when walking was much easier because the grasses had died off and the low willows and the thick alders had lost their leaves, so he could see where he was stepping. And of course he always wore rubber chest waders then and he wasn't soaked and cold as he was now sloshing along the stream.

He came to the riverbank through a stand of young cottonwood trees and slid down a low sloping bank onto the gravel bar of a long straight run that he and his fishing friends called Dolly Land for the numerous small Dolly Varden char it used to hold. But the river had straightened in recent years and the holding water had filled in with gravel, and the Dollies no longer held there, and his friends were all gone too now. Gone to troubles of their own, troubles not all that different from Alan's. Except, of course, he was pretty sure that none of them had ended up killing anyone.

Down in the river among the heavy cottonwoods, he could no longer hear sirens on the roads above. He walked along the gravel bar in silence, up to his ankles in the shallows—hopefully that would confuse the police dogs—heading downstream only because that stretch of river was most familiar, and he knew the places where he'd have to get out and bushwhack through the woods around the worst log jams and sweepers. He walked, wondering what the police were doing, what Angela had explained to them. They would know he had the gun, but could they tell which direction he'd gone? Had Angela or one of the medics from the ambulance seen him slip into the alders along the driveway? If not, they wouldn't have any way of knowing where to start looking until the dogs picked up his trail. They would shut down the roads, both the highway and the secondary road to his subdivision. There was nothing to do now but keep walking to stave off the chill that was spreading from his wet legs to the rest of him. He should have grabbed his fishing jacket on the way out, but he'd thought he would be taking Angela's Firebird at that time. He walked faster, slipping and tripping on the rounded stones littering the shallows.

A mile or so downstream, probably halfway to the old iron bridge and the road, he was forced inland and into an alder thicket to get around a deep stretch, and he stumbled into an iron frying pan hanging from a low branch. Beneath it on the ground was a hatchet lying alongside a small fire pit. Alan smiled. This was the work of young boys playing at adventure by camping in this wet ugly thicket. He knew because it was the kind of inhospitable place he used to make camps when he was ten or twelve, pretending to be exploring wild new realms in the natural world. He and his brother Johnny would fry baloney and cook Campbell's Scotch Broth soup on hideously smoky wood fires. They'd smoke their mother's pur-loined Virginia Slims and peruse the magazines they filched from their father's chest of drawers. Johnny had died at forty. It was only five years ago, but it was also nearly 4,000 miles away and Alan hadn't seen his brother for years before he died. That was another thing you got used to, living in Alaska. Now, Alan realized that he had already forgotten what his brother's cause of death was, which ailment. He was simply too wrapped up in his own medical night-mares to keep track of what was killing others.

A cold, wet hour later the moon was low in the sky and setting, but still bright as he rounded a familiar bend and knew that the bridge was just downstream. He shivered, simultaneously over-heated from walking and chilled by his now-soaked clothes. He was so thirsty he finally gave up all caution and knelt and drank from the river with cupped hands. A little intestinal disruption seemed unimportant compared to everything else right then.

When he came around the last bend, exhausted, shivering, and almost ready to lie down and go to sleep in the willows, he was only half surprised to see a large SUV parked up on the bridge, idling there with a clear view of the river. With the vehicle mostly hidden by the shadows of the bridge structure he could only make out one word: Troopers. He stepped back into the willows and pulled the pistol out of his waistband. There were three bullets left in the cylinder. He flipped it open and pulled all three out and threw them into the river.

Holding the gun well apart from his body, where it could easily be seen, he stepped out of the shadowy forest and into bright moonlight on the gravel bar along the deep pool just above the bridge. Someone shouted and he heard car doors opening and slamming. More shouting. Bright searchlights flooded the gravel bar, throwing stark shadows behind every low bush and plant.

Shivering uncontrollably now, Alan stopped within fifty feet of the bridge, within fifty feet of the searchlights and the troopers. He stood staring at the surface of the river, itself quivering in the floodlights. He didn't think about Angela and her brother Dace. He didn't think about the moose calf. There was nothing more he could do for them. He thought about the river.

How many times he had fished here? Right here in the Bridge Hole? He'd caught king salmon here every Memorial Day weekend for years, back when there were still enough kings running in the river to allow a fishing season. Silver salmon too, in late summer. And his fall favorite, steelhead. All those fish. All those years. They were right there with him at the edge of the water now. But what was he doing here without his fishing tackle or waders? What was he doing here holding a gun in his hand? What was he doing here?

Too tired to figure that out, his brain spinning, heart fluttering madly again, every muscle in his body aching from the bushwhacking hike along the river, it exhausted him just thinking of how many hours he'd spent walking and fishing this river over the past thirty years. But that was nothing compared to how much of those same years he'd spent *not* fishing. The tiresome hours spent working a job he'd never been good at, the troubling hours spent fighting with Gwen, the frightening hours spent sitting in doctors' offices or lying in hospital beds.

The troopers called out to him by name, and he looked up into the blinding lights. A voice from behind the lights spoke through a megaphone offering him something. He could hear reason in the voice and knew there was a way out all this, if he went through the motions that would require. He stood there for the longest time. But this was time well spent—time on the water, as he'd promised himself. Still, sooner or later you have to move. You have to do the next thing.

"Alan?" the voice said.

Squinting up into the floodlights, Alan got control of the shivering. "Yes," he said, "I'm here." And he raised the big pistol and pointed it at the police.

Chekhov's Rule

When I first met Walker two years ago, he had a job at the tackle shop on the river, a valid driver's license, and a classic early '70s Chevy Nova, competition orange. He still had all his teeth. Now the job, the car, his license, and half his teeth are gone, and he's on disability, like two-thirds of the people around here.

Half his teeth. Two-thirds of the people. Something about this place makes me think in fractions. Nothing feels whole anymore.

Don't ask me what Walker's so-called disability is. The inability to chew solid foods or hold a job? I don't mean to sound harsh—my wife Janine says I'm not a generous person—but every life has its ups and downs. Around here the highs seem to happen early and die quickly. And the only way they ever come back again is in a bottle, a needle, or a pipe.

It was Janine's idea to move here. When she saw the job opening at the hospital in the town on the bay, she squealed, "Alaska!" The romance of the far north had her by the heartstrings and set her house hunting. She would've gone for a yurt in the middle of a swamp if I hadn't insisted on four solid walls and running water. We've been here two years now, and she's more at home every day. Me? I can feel the hunger out there. This place is getting ready to eat us.

But back to Walker.

This morning I was driving to the post office to pick up our mail when I saw him down in the ditch alongside the road, wading through knee-deep snow, mouth frozen in that toothless pink smile of his, eyes all over the place. He was wearing a long dark coat, and—although it was January and maybe 20° and snowing again—no hat. The borough snowplows had left berms like mountain ranges along both shoulders, and I guess he didn't want to take his chances walking in the road, which is reptile curvy and barely wide enough for two cars. Walker is off a couple notches, for sure, but not stupid. Trust me, crazy and stupid are sometimes two entirely different things. I wondered why he wasn't driving the four-wheeler that had replaced his Chevy.

With fresh snow on black ice, I drove slowly. Over the top of the berm, I recognized his curly black hair plastered with flakes, his silver sideburns, those two-tone eyebrows of his. The premature gray makes it hard to tell how old he is. Late thirties I'd guess if I had to. Yet in spite of that, and the missing teeth, it's amazing how handsome Walker remains. Picture a young Mel Gibson. Only crazier.

Since Janine and I moved here, I've tried to stay cordial with the locals—it's cheap insurance—so I honked my horn. Walker kept walking as if he didn't hear it, smiling like he loved post-holing through heavy snow up to his zipper. Without turning my way, he waved one hand high overhead, something big and shiny in his grip. I was already past him when I realized it was an enormous pistol.

Maybe I should've turned around and gone back, offered him a lift, tried to stop him from whatever mayhem he intended with that. But I can't fix what's wrong with these people, I told myself. Plus, sanity is not a requirement for gun ownership in this state—or any other, as far as I know. I kept driving.

It was the first time I'd seen him in months. Frankly, I'd been hoping he'd moved. I didn't care where he went or why. The last time I talked to him was back in October, when he showed up at our house looking for one of his wayward semi-feral cats. He has six or eight of the things living with him in a little shack cobbled onto a derelict travel trailer. The place is set back fifty yards off the road on a two-track through the alders. A wood stove for heat, no running water. The property is owned by a very old woman, Mrs. Grackly, who lives nearby in another shack almost as rough. They're two miles from us by the winding road. A lot closer if you cut directly through the woods to our house.

Walker is supposed to take care of the old gal as a way of paying rent. People around here have all kinds of deals like that going. Anything to avoid real work. Janine was Mrs. Grackly's nurse at the hospital for a while last summer. That's how she met the old woman. Now Janine brings her food and makes sure she has firewood and water. Never mind that Walker is supposed to be doing that. That's my wife all over. Helping people in need and enabling those who pretend to be.

* * *

It was a warm fall evening when Walker came looking for his cat, the birch trees gone bright yellow, the sky all pink behind the dead volcanoes across the bay. The kind of night that could almost make a person love this place. Walker pulled up in the driveway on his four-wheeler. Of course, you're not supposed to drive ATVs on state roads. But if the police enforced that, half the people around here would starve to death in their own homes.

Janine and I were eating dinner. We went out on the porch to see what he wanted. She was always trying to help him with his cats. She wasn't aware that I knew she bought bags of kibble and dropped them off at his place. And sometimes food for him too, as if he were a hungry animal or an old sick person like Mrs. Grackly. Lost animals. Lost souls. Janine can't resist providing what she thinks people need. More than once I've had to convince myself that what she feels for me is love, not pity. That's a hell of a distinction for a man to have to make.

"Hi, Walker," Janine said. "Who'd you lose now? Gray Guy? Paddlefoot?"

How she could remember the names of someone else's pets is beyond me. If we had children I'd need them to wear name tags.

"Where's the Nova?" I asked him, before this turned into a whole conversation about cats.

"Gone," he said, still sitting on the idling four-wheeler.

"Jeez, if I knew you wanted to sell it—"

But then his cat—whatever its name was—an orange longhair with a tail the size of a push broom, squirmed out from under our porch, ran over, and jumped up into Walker's lap. He hugged the animal so hard I thought its eyes would pop out.

Janine leaned over the railing. "How are you, Walker?" she asked. "How're you doing?"

Walker rubbed his black and white mustache against the top of the cat's head and kind of shrugged, eyes darting my way for a second. I thought he looked like he wanted to answer that—but not with me there on the porch next to her.

"Dinner's getting cold," I said, and went back inside and repositioned my chair so I could see the porch from the table. Janine stayed right there. I ate my cold dinner, wondering what had happened to his classic Chevy, watching them talk, my wife leaning over the railing, pointing her beautiful butt my way, and Walker holding a giant cat on his lap and laughing with her. I'm not proud of where those two thoughts led me.

* * *

But back to Walker in the ditch by the side of the road.

He was slouching forward into the snowdrifts like a Neanderthal hunter. Waving that big handgun around. Not a hunting rifle or a shotgun—a pistol. First of all, nobody hunts in the middle of winter. And second, there is only one kind of animal anybody hunts with a pistol, at any time of year.

A while back it occurred to me that I was probably the only man in Alaska who didn't own a firearm. I'll admit that I was a little proud of that. It was a matter of principle, something that set me apart from the others around here. But it was beginning to seem simply unwise. Now I'm just like everyone else, a true local. Except, so far, I haven't yet felt the urge to join in the widespread shooting of road signs or rusting kitchen appliances, a kind of tradition in these parts.

Anyway, I picked up our mail and drove back home through the falling snow, wondering if I would find him still slogging through the drifts in the ditch, carrying that gun. But he was nowhere around when I made the turn off the pavement onto our snowed-over side road. He could've cut in through the woods anywhere, depending on where he was going with the pistol. God, did I even want to know?

When I got home I turned on the local public station for the news, waiting to hear who'd been shot around here that morning. It happens more often than you'd think for a town this small. Janine was working at the hospital, fifteen miles away, wouldn't be home until 5:00 or so. It was snowing harder, and the driveway needed clearing. I should've been out running the snowblower. But I stayed inside and paced the house the rest of the day, letting the snow accumulate and thinking about him out there somewhere armed with a pistol the size of a rocket launcher. He had no reason to do me harm, I told myself. Several times.

At 5:00 I put out some snacks for Janine. It's a ritual we have. I work at home—I'm translating a book by a Russian poet nobody's ever heard of—and out here in the woods, there isn't anyone to talk to all day. Honestly, I don't see myself making lots of friends here anytime soon. So it's kind of a big deal for me when Janine comes home. I like to have something ready to munch on. I like to fix her a drink.

I cut up some hard salami, put out some olives and chunks of smoked salmon on a plate, and started watching the clock. By 5:30 I'd called her twice. Went straight to message. Her phone was off. Why would she turn her phone off if she was done working her shift?

Outside the forest around the house was going dark. There was no wind, and the falling snowflakes filtered down in slow motion through the dense shadows of the alder thickets. It got darker and darker. One reason I agreed to move to Alaska is because it's the most like Russia of anyplace on American soil. I feel immersed in winter here on snowy days like this, and it puts me more in touch with the writers I'm translating. This is my Siberia, and I'd like to think it makes my writing authentic and somehow more important. But I'd be lying if I said there isn't a kind of cold loneliness to it too. Chekhov called winter "evil, dark, and long." I tried not to think about that as I dialed Janine's phone again. Nothing.

I switched the porch lights on and poured myself a Jameson's and sat at the table by the window watching the untouched driveway—like I could make her appear there by staring at it. All the stories she brought home from the emergency room started unspooling in my brain. The crazy bastard who took a bullet in the stomach when he asked his wife to shoot a pair of handcuffs off his wrists. The six-year-old boy whose stepfather burned his hair off with a "hillbilly flame thrower" made from a spray can of engine starter and a Bic. Some drug dealer with one eye shot out—by a bow and arrow, of all things. The shit these people do to each other amazes me. You don't need to read the Russians to find insane cruelty and mayhem.

One of the older nurses told Janine, "Oh, it used to be a lot worse back in the meth days. With everyone on heroin now, they're more likely to kill themselves than anybody else."

I try to find some comfort in that.

*　*　*

At 6:00 it was fully dark, and I was really getting twitchy, thinking about driving toward town to see if her Subaru was in a ditch. Then I heard the growling of a four-wheeler engine. I looked out the window to see small close-together headlights crawling up our driveway like some awful bright-eyed winter insect approaching. Janine was riding on the back of Walker's machine, arms hugged around him as they plowed through the drifts. When he stopped at the foot of our porch stairs, she was laughing so hard she slid off the rig and landed in the snow. More laughing. Not from me, mind you.

She stood and dusted the snow off her pants. Walker smiled, that skunk-striped mustache shining in the porch lights. He still had his trench coat on, still no hat. No sign of that big handgun now. I looked for that. He glanced up at me standing in the window, trained his squirrely eyes on me, gave me his gummy smile, and turned the machine back down the driveway. Janine stomped up the snowy stairs and into the house.

*　*　*

She'd stopped to look in on Old Lady Grackly, she told me, couldn't restart her car when she came out. Dead battery. "Luckily," as she put it, luckily Walker was there to give her a ride home on his four-wheeler.

"Why didn't you call?"

Her phone was dead too. Neither Walker nor the old lady had a phone of any kind. Of course.

"The car battery *and* your phone battery are both dead?" I scoffed. "You better check your vibrator."

"Hah," Janine said, and climbed out of her snowy boots. "Some days are like that."

Yes, I thought, more and more of them, all the time.

"Yeah, thank God for Walker," I said, really pissed that while I was worried sick about her, she was out there riding around pressed up against him on his four-wheeler.

Janine gave me a look. "Why don't you like him?"

"I saw him walking in the ditch along the road today," I said, "carrying a gun."

"I know. He told me he saw you drive by. He was on his way to get his four-wheeler back from the Pakula kid."

"The Pakula kid. Jesus." This just keeps getting better. "That one's out of jail again?"

"Rehab," she corrected me.

"How encouraging. Was anybody killed?"

"It didn't come to that," Janine said, reaching for a piece of salami.

"Well, I'm glad it didn't come to that." My head felt thick, like my brain was freezing or something. "Do you and Walker have long conversations about his lowlife associates?"

Janine chewed her salami and took a glass out of the cupboard. She pulled the vodka out of the freezer and poured, letting me wait for an answer that never came. She cut a lemon wedge, plopped it in, splashed some soda water on top. She tasted it. "Will you take me to Mrs. Grackly's and jump-start the car in the morning?"

"Of course," I said, feeling morally exquisite. That is to say, the injured party. Though I wasn't sure how I'd been injured.

She picked up the snacks and her drink and stopped. "You know, it would have been nice if you'd at least offered him a ride this morning. Or even just asked if he was okay. It wouldn't hurt to be a little neighborly once in a while."

She waited for a second to see if I was going to argue with that.

How could I argue with that?

"I see," she said to herself and went upstairs. I heard the bathtub running. For someone who was in love with the idea of roughing it in Alaska, Janine spends a hell of a lot of time in that bathtub.

"Plug your phone in, please," I shouted up the stairs after her.

"Thank you for reminding me," came back down.

Believe me, any time an evening starts out this politely, you can be sure it's going to be evil, dark, and long.

* * *

Everybody knows that Chekhov said that if a gun appears in the first act of a play, a gun has to go off in the third act. I don't think he ever said it has to be the same gun.

It has stopped snowing now.

Walker's out there somewhere. Toothless, crazy, and heavily armed. I'm sure of it. And I'm ready. There are still months of winter left to go. Months and months.

This is life here in my private Siberia. You want it? Let me know.

Mammoth

It was their first big trip together, and their first big argument as a couple. About the food.

Jack wanted to bring nothing but instant soups and oatmeal, energy bars and the freeze-dried meal packets he's brought on fishing and hunting trips since he was a boy. The kinds of things you're *supposed* to bring when back-country camping in Alaska.

Mary proposed freezing her homemade soups and stews, spaghetti sauce, chili. She planned to bring whole meals in Tupperware boxes. She wanted to pack fresh vegetables and fruits. Salad supplies.

Salads!

Jack scoffed and blurted something snotty about "farmers' market food-zombies paying too much for everything they put in their mouths." He saw her pained look and tried to smooth it over. "Mary, seriously, weight is an issue in a collapsible rubber canoe. You want to sink us?"

"I can't eat freeze-dried food for two weeks, Jack. I doubt anyone can . . . and survive." She raised her eyebrows with finality. "How about we take turns cooking every other day?"

We're still getting to know each other, Jack told himself. And the meals he'd had at Mary's apartment had been spectacular. "Fine," he said. "Bring a whole restaurant if you want. But only what fits into one cooler."

"Deal," she said.

"A small cooler. Please? It's a camping trip, not a picnic."

Jack told his older brother about their plans, and his brother smiled. "Good for you, Jackie. You're finally learning how to behave in a relationship. Each side contributes at least half. Good for you."

Jack had gone through several decidedly short-term girlfriends, their departures nearly always their idea, and always attributed to some variation of his selfish and/or controlling behavior. He was pleased about his apparently enlightened decision to let Mary bring half the food—until they checked in for their jet from Anchorage to Kotzebue. Her massive cooler weighed three ounces under the Alaska Airlines fifty-pound weight limit. It was barely going to fit between the gunwales of the canoe.

Mary grinned triumphantly. "Dang, I could've brought another two ounces of chicken stock."

Jack grimaced, hoping it looked like a smile.

*　　*　　*

It's late afternoon their third day on the river, and Mary's turn to cook. Frankly, Jack is glad. Last night he stirred packets of instant split pea and instant French onion soup mixes together and poured it over a bowl of freeze-dried rice. His signature camping dish. He's wowed a lot of hunting and fishing buddies with that one. Mary was less than impressed. And coming on the heels of the home-made pumpkin raviolis she'd served the first night, he'd have to admit his culinary concoction didn't seem quite as delectable as he remembered it.

Now he's a quarter mile from their camp casting a fly under a thick piece of driftwood that arches over a little snowmelt feeder stream. He looks back downstream at their tent, pitched in the ver-dant willows where the stream enters the Noatak. On the other side of the big river a remnant snowfield glistens blue-white under the summer solstice sun. A thin column of gray smoke rises into the windless air. Mary has been simmering red beans on a twig fire all day because Jack—he was truly horrified that she'd brought dried beans instead of something instant—had said they'd take too much time to cook on the camp stove. "Our propane has to last two weeks."

"I know how to build a fire," she'd said.

"Okay, but firewood's kind of scarce at this elevation, this far above the Arctic Circle. Look around. You see any trees?"

It's true—at this elevation, at this latitude—nothing grows but hip-high willows and spindly alders. Tundra mosses, arctic cotton, and low berry bushes stretch from the river corridor to the still-snowy hilltops. Since midafternoon Mary has been feeding twigs and beaver cuttings into her fire under Jack's now thoroughly blackened lightweight cook pot.

Jack is about to cast the fly up against the big driftwood log again when it dawns on him that the hefty log curving up out of the gravel like the Golden Arches of fast-food fame is all wrong there. At least five inches in diameter and four feet long, it's as incongruous on the treeless landscape as an actual McDonalds would be. How can there be a branch that size if there are no trees?

That stops him mid-cast, the airborne fly line collapsing around him as he realizes what he's looking at. He knows what it is. And he knows he's going to keep it.

* * *

Lumbering into camp with his heavy prize crushing his shoulder, he drops the thing onto the gravel next to the canoe with a thud. Mary looks up from the fire. "Oh, my God," she says. "Do you know what that is?"

"Sure. It's almost stone now and weighs a ton, as hard and dry as those beans you've been cooking all day. But it was a tusk." He leans his fly rod against the tent. "Still is, I guess. Fossil ivory?" The aroma of the bubbling beans wafts to his nostrils. His stomach twists. "Are those ready? I'm starving."

"I'll bet you are, after a hard day hunting Pleistocene megafauna." He laughs. "And with nothing but a fly rod."

"Yes, the hard dry beans are ready." Mary frowns quizzically. "Why did you drag that thing back here? You know it's illegal to remove fossils from public lands. This whole river is in a federal preserve."

"Mary, it's thousands of years old!"

"Tens of thousands maybe," she corrects him.

"That's what I mean," Jack says. "Someone should see it."

"Jack," Mary says, and sighs. "*We've* seen it." She looks to see if he's going to respond to that.

He has just enough sense not to.

She reaches for the camp stove. "I'll start the rice."

*　*　*

She's quiet as they eat the flavorful Cajun-style beans and rice. Her nearly fifty-pound ice chest was hell to portage through the willows down to the river from the little pingo lake where the float plane dropped them off. But her meals are heaven.

"Delicious," he says and means it. "Man!"

"Thank you." She looks over at the tusk. "Jack, be reasonable. You're not really going to put that thing in the canoe, are you? It must weigh a hundred pounds."

"Absolutely delicious." Jack shovels more beans and rice into his mouth. "Pass the Tabasco please?"

Mary groans, "You Paleolithic hunters are so thick-skulled."

"Oog," he says.

*　*　*

After dinner they open the Nalgene bottle of Tullamore Dew, Jack's one concession to packing liquids. It's late, but the sun is still circling the arctic sky on its elliptical summer solstice path. Mary sips her whiskey and stares past the tusk and across the river. "God, imagine ancient people camping right here, eating their dinner and looking up to see one of those shaggy elephants fording the river."

Her eyes are glassy, and Jack can tell that she's seeing the huge animals as clearly as if they really are there. Her imagination is what he liked about her when they first met at the museum in Anchorage. Jack's brother, the family professor, had dragged him there for a fundraiser for some land trust or something. Jack had resisted.

"Come on," his brother said. "You might meet a nice eco–cutie pie."

"Is my desperation that obvious?"

His brother shook his head. "It's like an aura around you, kid."

Jack had to admit that the event wasn't horrible. There was a talk about habitat loss in coastal wetlands, and Jack listened attentively. This crowd certainly included some who would cringe at the thought of shooting animals, but duck hunters like Jack were a powerful constituency for habitat protection. Even so, his camo cap stood out among the wool Sherpa hats and Nature Conservancy caps. These were well-meaning people, doing seriously good work to save the outdoor world that he loved as much as they did, if for different uses. Jack could see that. Even so, once the presentation was over, the self-congratulatory camaraderie began to smother him. He wandered away from the wine and cheese table and went to look at the display cases of ancient Alaskan hunting weapons, frankly incredulous that anyone could feed his family with tools like those. Spears? Bows and arrows? He had a hard enough time bringing home game using high-powered rifles and shotguns.

He was still considering all that when a woman's voice came from behind him. "Don't those atlatls make you just want to travel back in time and hunt something big and woolly?"

"You must be on one of those Paleo diets," Jack joked. He turned to face her, expecting one of his brother's female students, some over-earnest mouse-haired intellectual in a tweedy zippered sweater and matching skirt. Birkenstocks over wool socks.

And there was Mary, an archeologist and expert on early tools—hair in blinding yellow braids, cheeks flushed—gazing at the display case in near-delirious wonder. In her knee-tattered Carhartt bibs and Xtratuf boots, she looked like she'd just split a cord of birch or put snow chains on her truck.

Wonder. That's the word for her approach to life. Though she has twice the education he does, there's a charming girlish goofiness to her enthusiasm about everything she hurls herself into. Not just food and cooking. Or sex. Although *those* go in the plus column, for sure. But everything she even thinks. Every opinion. Every idea. The woman doesn't do lukewarm.

Now she's squinting across the Noatak as if she's really expecting woolly rhinos or giant sabre-toothed cats to materialize on the snowfield. "Imagine," she says again.

"That's what I mean," Jack says. "It's so old, so rare. I couldn't just leave it out there."

She sighs, still in her whimsical daze. "Did you know that the last mammoths died out just 4,000 years ago on Wrangel Island? It's not that far from here. Scientists think rising sea levels made the water table too salty to drink." Her voice has gone sad. "Climate change," she intones in the hushed near whisper his Irish grandmother used for words like "divorce" or "Protestant."

"Climate change? Four thousand years ago?" he blurts. He knows better than to tease her about this, but he can't stop himself. "From what? All those oil-fired power plants the Egyptians built? Takes a lot of electricity to light up a pyramid, I guess."

She looks at him like she doesn't know who, or even *what*, he is. That's the downside of her charm; it bruises so quickly. They finish their whiskey in silence. Though it's evening, the sun is still high in the sky—this far north it won't set for another couple weeks—but when clouds move across it the temperature falls. A cool wind rolls up the river. It feels like it came all the way from the Bering Sea, many miles downstream.

"I'm going to turn in," she says neutrally. If she's angry, she's keeping a lid on it.

They brush their teeth and crawl into the new sleeping bags Jack bought for the trip because they can be zipped together. This is the first time he's ever camped with anyone he wanted in his bag with him.

The bedrolls are the first things they'll own together as a couple. If that's what they are.

"Great dinner," he says, nuzzling her ear.

"Egyptians," she says, and rolls away.

* * *

The next morning dawns clear and sunny again. Mary is cordial, but still quiet. She's cooking oatmeal on the camp stove—not the instant packets Jack has eaten on every camping trip of his life—actual steel-cut oats. He wants to point out that, like the beans, those take a lot more time and therefore more fuel to cook, but he's feeling bad about the climate change crack. And besides, she's brought a tiny bottle of pure maple syrup to drizzle on the oatmeal. He eats like a cave dweller, says nothing.

His father used to say to Jack and his brother, "Find yourself girls who can cook, boys." Then he'd wink. "Everything else you can do for yourself." The only time Jack could remember his father preparing a meal was the night his mother was in the hospital delivering their baby sister. "Looks like it's just us men," his father said. He clipped the end off a plastic package of hot dogs, held it above his face, and drank the stream of cloudy liquid they were packed in. Wiping his mouth with the back of his hand, he chopped the franks up and dumped them into some boiling pasta. "I call this 'Daddy noodles,'" he said proudly. Then he paused. "Maybe we don't mention it to your mother, eh, boys? Tomorrow night we'll eat at the bar. Promise."

They finish breakfast and decide to spend the morning there at the mouth of the creek. Jack wants to explore the little stream farther up into the moraine of the receding ice sheet that feeds it. He picks up his fly rod. "I'll try to get some grayling for lunch. You want to come for a hike?"

Mary shakes her head. "I'm going to bake camp biscuits." She pulls his now-scorched pot from the cook supplies along with a bag of flour.

He can tell she's not over his stupid remark. For him climate change is an issue like social injustice or any other of the numerous and constant threats menacing life on earth. Racism, wars, famines, floods, droughts, religious fanatics. Worrisome, but remote. Only vaguely connected to his life. He donates to Ducks Unlimited, Trout Unlimited. He recycles—when he thinks of it. What more can he really do? For Mary it's intensely personal, like everything else. Nothing to joke about. He's hoping a few hours in the sunshine will warm her up.

"You okay?" he asks.

"It's going to take a while to make coals with the skimpy fire-wood," she says and walks away, gathering sticks.

"Look, I'm sorry about the Egyptian joke," he calls out.

She continues to pick beaver cuttings and small branches off the gravel but stops and gives him a half smile. "Go fish."

*　*　*

At this elevation the creeks are almost sterile, basically liquid ice. If salmon run this far up the river, they aren't there yet. There aren't many riparian insects either and no baitfish at all. Even arctic char are absent. He returns to camp hours later with nothing, and so they eat biscuits with peanut butter. After the long walk, the biscuits—baked perfectly golden and still warm from the cook pot—are the best thing Jack has ever tasted. He tells Mary again how good her food is. She thanks him but is still cool.

"I'm a piss-poor hunter-gatherer," he says.

She smiles to herself. "That had to be hard."

That's Mary too: empathy for everybody. Even people dead for a couple millennia.

The real question is, How long will it take her to figure out she's too good for him? He doesn't want to think about that.

Their comments on Paleolithic life have brought the subject of that fossil tusk to Jack's mind. And to Mary's too, he's pretty sure.

She peers downriver, clearly avoiding looking at the thing on the ground between them. "How far do you think we should float today?" she asks.

Jack takes out the map, happy for the diversion. They decide on a place where the river passes within hiking distance of a small lake. "Maybe I can get a lake trout or a pike for dinner."

He almost makes another joke but has the good sense to hold it.

"That would be nice," she says. "Sure."

It's Jack's night to cook. The prospect of having fresh fish to augment whatever freeze-dried meal he's planning seems to cheer her. But they have to step over and around the tusk as they break camp. There isn't a lot of idle chatter. None, actually.

When the canoe is packed and ready to launch, Jack hesitates and looks at Mary. Then he hefts the tusk onto the top of her cooler. Straps it down.

Mary pulls her life jacket on and speaks for the first time in a while. "Are you sure about this, Jack?"

Jack's anything but sure about this. Aside from the legal questions, the tusk, piled on top that way, gives their load a high center of gravity that's a very bad idea for an already overloaded canoe in moving water. In any water. That much he's sure about. If they get into rough water things could get ugly. But he can picture the fossil ivory cleaned up and polished, mounted on a varnished wood stand in his living room. In *their* living room someday. Maybe. If there is still a "them" two weeks from now and 200 miles downstream.

Mary's gone wistful again. "It could be 15,000 years old, maybe 20,000. It belongs here." She looks around at the endless wild country on all sides of them. A falcon soars past overhead. A ground squirrel shrills in alarm nearby. "Here," she says again, "in its place on the land."

"I know," he says. "But it would be a nice memento of our trip. Don't you think?"

"A memento?" She smiles at his attempt at romance. "Okay, we'll talk about it later," she says. "It's a very long river."

*   *   *

This stretch of the Noatak is wide and shallow. No rapids. No tricky water. Not a river that attracts whitewater adrenaline fiends. The allure of it is the vast unpopulated wilderness it flows through for over 400 miles. Now the sun is shining, the river whispering its mesmerizing story as they float along into the afternoon. Jack daydreams, dipping his paddle absently. Once again, he imagines the tusk mounted, but this time in a display case in the museum. He could say he found it someplace outside the preserve. "Donated by Mr. J. E. Donovan." That would make Mary proud. He hopes.

He's jarred back to attention when the canoe picks up speed as the river narrows and enters an S-shape bend he'd seen on the map. Nothing treacherous, just faster water for a quarter mile or so. He calls out, "Mary, when the river straightens again, I think the place we want to camp is just downstream on the left."

On his last word, the canoe jerks to a sudden halt. He's thrown forward and catches himself on the gear bags piled at his knees.

Mary lets out a shriek. "What's happening?"

They've gone aground on a boulder lying just below the surface. The rock is jammed under the hull amidship, the canoe pinned to it. Jack would be happier if the weight anchoring them there could be blamed solely on Mary's ice chest, but the tusk is twice as heavy as that, and he knows it.

The boulder is the size of a Volkswagen and as out of place in the otherwise pebbled river bottom as the tusk was in the little creek that far above the tree line. Luckily, it's been smoothed and nearly polished for who knows how many thousands of years by the glaciers that deposited it there. It didn't puncture the synthetic rubber skin of the canoe. But the flexible belly of the boat grips the top of the rock like it's glued to it. They're dead in the water. The river swirls around them, too deep to stand in and walk the canoe off its perch. It's not a life-threatening situation. Yet.

Mary turns in her seat, eyes wide. "What'll we do?"

He can't tell whether she's terrified or delighted. Maybe both. "Hang on. I'll try to rock us off it."

He lays the paddle across the gunwales and rocks the canoe. It wobbles side to side but doesn't shift. He knows what he has to do. "Hold tight," he says, and crawls forward over their gear bags and undoes the strap holding the tusk to the top of the cooler. Mary turns in her seat and watches him.

"Jack, wait. Do you have to?" Her face is taut, brow furrowed. "I know you really want that thing."

"What I really want is to get off this rock before it wears a hole in the rubber hull."

He reaches for the heavy fossil, thinking he can shove it ahead toward Mary to put the weight forward. Maybe that will pull the boat off the rock, and he can still keep the tusk. When he feels the canoe start to move, he almost chirps with victory. But with his weight off the stern, instead of sliding ahead the canoe pivots on the boulder like a weathervane. Broadside to the current it rolls, dumping them into the river.

They're both wearing life jackets and aren't going to drown. The job now is to get to shore and see what they've lost. Mary is already hanging onto the overturned canoe and kicking toward a long flat gravel bar on the left. A good person to know in a pinch, it's clear. Jack swims to catch up with her. Together they drag the canoe through the shallows to shore and right it.

There's good news and bad.

They both saved their paddles. Their gear and dry bags are securely lashed in. Mary's cooler is still tied to a thwart by its handles. All good.

The bad news is, upside down, the lid on the cooler popped open. Now brightly colored Tupperware boxes bob downstream like toy boats and disappear around a curve. Almost everything she brought—half their food—is gone. And still twelve days to go before the pilot meets them at the pickup point, miles downriver. They haven't seen anyone since they portaged over to the river and assembled the canoe. Haven't even seen or heard another plane pass overhead for three days. Jack had eschewed bringing a satellite phone. How many rivers has he floated, how many years has he done these kinds of trips before that technology was invented?

Well, they wanted something wild and remote for their first big trip together.

The sky is darkening, rain clouds building over the Brooks Range to the north. The air temp crashes as if someone flipped a switch.

"Let's pull everything up to the willows." He points. "If it rains in the headwaters, the river can rise fast. We don't want to wake up with it running through the tent."

Mary puts one hand on his arm. "Jack, I'm sorry about your fossil."

He looks to see if she's being sarcastic. She's not. "Sorry about your food," he says.

"Yeah, half our meals are gone." It's hard to tell if she's concerned about going hungry, or simply dreading having to eat his freeze-dried entrées every day.

"Okay, don't worry about that right now. We need to get out of these wet clothes."

By the time they haul everything to higher ground, change into dry clothes, and secure the tent to the willows, the sky is black. The bushes shudder, leaves thrashing belly-up on the rising gusts. Little spirals of dust dance across the gravel bar.

In the lee of the tent Jack starts the stove and puts water on to boil. A hot drink will cheer them up. He takes inventory. There are still packets of Knorr and Lipton soups, instant oatmeal, Mountain House freeze-dried dinners—enough for every other day. He looks up to see Mary watching him. "We won't starve," he says. "But we'll need to ration."

"You'll just have to catch fish."

She's not saying anything about whose fault this is. Yes, her cooler was heavy. But not that heavy. Without the tusk they would have gone right over the top of that sunken boulder.

He studies her face again. She's not going to say it.

"Yeah, fishing will get better further downriver," he says. "That lake I showed you on the map is just over this hill. When the storm blows through, I'll hike up and look for lake trout." He knows what he needs to say. "I shouldn't have put that thing in the boat. It was too big."

"Big?" She scoffs. "It was mammoth!"

"We're going Ice Age, and you're making jokes?" That came out a little harsher than he meant it, but he lets it ride. If she wants to make this into a fight, so be it.

She opens her mouth to say something but hesitates. "Hey, look." She points toward the downstream end of the gravel bar. A bit of color shows in the slow water of a little slough there. "One of my boxes, I think." She strides off into the wind.

The tea kettle whistles, and Jack crouches and pours boiling water into two cups of instant hot cocoa. He watches her fish something out of the slough. She returns in a moment, beaming like she's just discovered gold. She holds up a small plastic box with three small lemons in it, another one filled with round white onions the size of grapes. "See? I can gather!"

"Lemons," he says, "and tiny onions." He hands her a hot cocoa. "I knew there was something I forgot to pack."

She grins. "We may have to ration, but it can still taste good. You catch a trout and I'll stuff it with some Meyer lemon slices and onions, wrap it in foil. We'll build a fire and bake it on the coals." Her face goes even brighter. "Ooh. I think I have some fresh sage in one of my bags."

"She brought fresh sage," he says, trying to smile.

She holds up a baggie of herbs, her face radiant. "Tarragon too." She waggles her eyebrows at him. The rising arctic wind blows her braids straight out behind her head like little wings. She looks like an angel in a wool watch cap.

He can only stand there.

She gets serious and says, "We've got a ways to go, Jack. But we're going to be all right. You know that, don't you?"

"Sure," he says, but over Mary's shoulder, downstream, he can see another bend in the long river ahead, nothing more. Still, he tells himself, so many others have done this before. What could go wrong? he asks himself. How hard can it be?

Uncommon Weather

What's on my mind, what I want to talk about, all happened last February, a month that used to mean bone-freezing winter this far north, but not anymore. All that afternoon warm Chinook winds bashed the cabin-turned-house my husband Herb and I have called home for twenty-two years. Unseasonable rain slashed the windows and drenched the sagging snow berms along the driveway. Still, Herb was out there in it, splitting firewood with the heavy maul.

Never mind that we had a brand-new oil-fired furnace—part of our plan to enjoy ourselves a little now that our twins, Megan and Joan, were off at college in Anchorage. We'd finally gotten running water, our first indoor toilet, a hot-water tank, a washer and dryer, and a pink fiberglass bathtub big enough for two. All the planet-destroying luxuries I'd always longed for. We figured we were due. Living all those years without. Before, if we had a carbon footprint at all, it would have shown five skinny toes and a naked heel. Now it was our turn not to give a shit.

Herb had finally hit the jackpot in the herring-roe fishery and decided that, with the girls gone, I might enjoy some creature comforts to take the edge off being alone in the cabin so much while he's away fishing. Unfortunately, I'd already come to that same conclusion, and one of the comforts I'd treated myself to was named Jimmy, a guy from my yoga class.

Although the affair had ended by February, there was Herb, standing out in the nearly tropical downpour in a wool shirt, splitting wood we didn't need to burn. You hear more and more these days about climate change, unusual storms all over the world. But let me tell you, it's the weather *inside* a house that matters.

I was at my new sink, finishing the dinner dishes, when Herb finally came in with an armload of spruce, rainwater seeping from the visor of his hat. He kicked the door shut behind him with his heel and went to the old wood stove we continued using to offset the expensive fuel oil the new furnace burned. He dropped the wood from chest height, turned and glared at me. I'd been trying to get him to talk all day, but I could only pry three words out of him, the only three words I'd heard pass his lips for a week.

"Herb," I said, "it's over. Really."

And Herb kind of wearily said, "Go fuck yourself."

Herb was never a big talker, but that was brief even for him.

He was between fishing runs. The gray-cod season had just ended, and halibut hadn't started yet. Or maybe it was the black cod that was ending and the herring about to begin again. I used to be able to keep track of it all, but one fish was pretty much the same as another to me anymore. The names of all the places Herb went in search of them had started to blur together too: the Gulf of Alaska, the Shelikof Straights, the Bering Sea. Places that have shaped our lives, places I have never seen. Even back when our daughters were small, it didn't really matter what Herb was fishing for or whether he was a mile offshore or a hundred; I wouldn't hear from him for weeks. The ship's radio was for emergencies, he said, and my being cooped up in a cabin in the woods with twin babies all winter was not, in his estimation, an emergency. And I suppose he was right. Although it was something. Something I don't recommend, by the way, whatever you choose to call it.

* * *

When the kids were six months old, Herb bought a huge boat. He named it the *Twin Angels* after the girls. He took it out scallop dragging in the Aleutians, and I didn't see him that whole winter. He did phone every couple weeks when they went into Dutch Harbor to offload. On the days he was supposed to call, I'd bundle the girls into the car and drive the ten miles to the pay phone in town in front of our little grocery store that hadn't yet become a big fancy Safeway. That was when winter was still winter. I'd wait in the bitter darkness, hopping from foot to foot like the local sea crows, trying to picture my husband out there on the stormy ocean somewhere, halfway to Korea.

After one of those calls, I was in the store warming up, picking through the unripe tomatoes we were stuck with in those days before reliable air freight, when I overheard the words "*Twin Angels.*" There were two young men at the apples, talking about fishing. One was a redhead and the other dark-eyed with dusty black dreadlocks and the first pierced nostril I'd ever seen in town, though many more would follow. The dreadlocked one said, "I thought you were scalloping with Herb."

"Fishery Division shut it down," the redhead said. "Some beef with the Japanese or something. Herb sent us home."

I stood there, my babies asleep in the shopping cart, a gray-green tomato clutched in my hand, and I listened to him say that the *Twin Angels* wasn't going back out to sea for three weeks at the earliest.

When I'd talked to Herb on the phone just minutes before this, he had not mentioned anything about having three weeks off. Or deciding to spend them out there in Dutch Harbor. I guess anything was better than being stuck in the cabin with me and two howling babies. I could understand that. Almost. You do what you have to do if you're a woman. If you're a man you do what you want to do.

I staggered to the register with that awful tomato in my grip, as if I believed it would somehow ripen on my windowsill in the constant gloom of winter. Still in a daze, I filled our five-gallon plastic jugs from the potable water spigot in front of the store. I was loading them into the car when I met a man.

I'm only five-foot-one and small boned. Five gallons of water is almost half my weight, and I was killing myself wrestling the heavy jugs into the hatchback of our old Subaru, with the thought of Herb staying out in Dutch—for reasons he had chosen not to share—spinning through my head. One of the water jugs got away from me and smashed a bag of rice cakes I was treating myself to, and I looked at them and started crying. You have to have lived the way we did back then to understand how sad a bag of smashed rice cakes can be. When a nice-looking guy walked up, took the water jug from my hand, and swung it into the car, I wiped my nose on my sleeve and smiled at him.

He was wearing Carhartt overalls and a watch cap. He had a clean beard and warm eyes. He smelled like soap. He said, "I hope you've got someone to unload this for you at home." But I knew that that was the very last thing he was hoping.

I thought about it for a second or two, still stung by Herb's decision not to come home. The girls were just babies and wouldn't know anything. And couldn't tell on me even if they did. I looked at the friendly guy. I thought about it a second longer. Then I shook my head and got in my car and drove off, flattered and flushed and a little proud of myself for leaving that good-looking man standing in the parking lot in the cold wind with nothing but a near miss to his credit and the crows pecking spilled rice cakes off the ice around his feet.

There is something to be said for being desired. I'm forty-six years old now, with lines in all the places you'd expect them and a chest as flat as the economy around here. But men are not as simple as they may seem, and sometimes a good smile is worth more than a blouse full of tits. Let's just say that I don't have any trouble making male friends—that guy Jimmy, for example. Let me *also* say that I didn't intend to hurt Herb. When I met Jimmy, I saw a lonely, desperate guy in need of a friend. I mean, really, a grown man taking a yoga class by himself is a cry for help if I ever saw one.

* * *

Herb stuffed wood into the stove. Between the roaring fire and the mild weather, the cabin was stifling. I put away the last of the dishes, mopped the sweat off my forehead with my apron, and took it off. Herb was still crouched at the open door of the stove, fussing with the fire.

"Come on, Herb," I said. "You're going to burn the place down."

Nothing.

"Seriously. Before you go back out again, we really need to talk."

"Okay, then," he said, "go fuck yourself."

That was his most complex sentence in days. Five words. At this rate it was going to be a very long evening.

Luckily, I had a hockey game. My best friend, Terri Destino, had talked me into joining the Kenai Peninsula Ladies League. She said it would keep me out of trouble, although there hadn't been dramatic results in that respect. That night we were playing the Cook Inlet Whales. Well, they aren't really the Whales. That's just what Terri named them. The team's real name is the Cook Inlet Lynxes. Terri started calling them the Whales because somehow all the biggest, heaviest women in this part of the world—the ones who can skate, at least—are on that one team. It's also no secret that the Whales refer to our team, the Peninsula Wildcats, as the Side Stripes, a type of local shrimp. Everyone on our team, me and Terri included, is as scrawny as a swizzle stick. Terri and I together weigh maybe 210 pounds carrying our skate bags, our hockey sticks, and the big thermos of vodka martinis we drink before every game.

I picked up my gear bag and headed for the cabin door. "Herb, honey," I said, "I'm going to the rink."

Herb prodded the fire and gave me a look like he wanted to bend the poker over my head. But Herb is a gentle soul and has never raised a hand to me or our girls, not even that terrible moment when I had to admit that it was true what he heard about me and Jimmy.

I reached for the door handle and said, "Terri and I are going out for pizza after the game. I may be late."

Herb opened his mouth, but before he could speak, I said, "Yes, honey. I know, 'Go fuck myself.' See you later, hon."

I stepped out of the sweltering cabin into the wet wind. It was only 6:00 but near dark already. However oddly mild the weather, it was still February, after all. Global warming may bring us a whole new earth, but the sun still rises and sets in its same old ways.

Rain was running over the ice on the steep slope of our driveway. Even with four studded tires, the Subaru basically free-fell to the road and ricocheted off the snow berm on the other side. I careened out into the paved road, praying there were no moose on it that night. Not for the first time, I tried to remember when this lifestyle in Alaska had last sounded like a good idea.

* * *

At the rink there was a good crowd, a nice turnout for a local game. People were getting used to the idea of being out among others again without having to wear masks and such. The Whales—big girls, every one of them—skated onto the ice for the national anthem. Terri elbowed me. "Look," she said, "the Thighs Capades."

That Terri has a way with words.

As usual the Whales kicked the living Jesus out of us. There was no way I could've faced them without Terri's thermos of Smirnoff and green olives. All I could do to keep them from skating right over the top of me was foul them constantly. In the first few minutes of the game I high-sticked Mary Godowski, clipped Ann Reston, and blatantly tripped Glenda Brevnik. Glenda slid headfirst into the boards, jumped back up, and punched me in the face with a fist like a canned ham. My gloves came off, and the crowd roared. How they love a girl fight. It took two refs to pry the furious Glenda off me.

I got into another fight later and spent more time in the penalty box. By the end of the second period I had a loose tooth and a nostril packed with Kleenex. But it paid off: the Whales' defense was keeping their distance from me, and I was wide open when, in the final minutes of the game—we were still scoreless—I caught a pass from Terri right in front of the Whales' goalie, Lucy Pevoworcek, the biggest player in the league.

Poor Lucy is *very* large, and I feel for her. I really do. I have seen her parked in front of the Safeway, wedged behind the wheel of her van, pushing sweet-and-sour chicken chunks into her mouth and then throwing the carton out the window so there will be no evidence when she arrives home with bags of healthy low-fat groceries lined up in the back. What else can she do? When people judge you for the things you desire, you start keeping secrets.

I faked right and Lucy spun that way and tangled her skates and went down like she'd been harpooned. I slapped the puck up and over her and into the net. The buzzer sounded. Our team went wild. We'd lost the game, but at least we were on the scoreboard for once. They mobbed me, pounding on me like we'd just clinched the Stanley Cup.

Even though the Whales had won 7 to 1, they disputed my goal, saying it went in after the buzzer, but Marty, the new young referee, sided with us. I thanked him with my friendliest smile. Marty responded with a grin that could've defrosted Antarctica. Terri caught our little exchange and glared at me with her tiny terrier face. More than once she has accused me of purposely racking up penalty minutes so I can sit in the box next to a certain great-looking but happily married timekeeper named Steve.

I do get a lot of penalties. It's true. But I can't help it. I get excited. I'm covered with padding and wearing a helmet. And when I'm on skates, I'm three inches taller than I've ever been in my life. It's very empowering. I have a half a thermos of vodka in my blood and a big wooden stick in my hands. Of course I'm going to start hitting people. And then there are those confusing rules about all those lines painted in the ice. The truth is I'm not good with rules. Ask my husband.

After the game I skidded through a sleet storm to the Aztec Boat House, a Mexican-Italian place on the bay overlooking the small boat harbor. They pour marinara sauce on cheese enchiladas and sell them as manicotti. The important thing is they have a full liquor license and stay open late.

I sat with Terri and our teammates Lauren Jones and Angela Sweeney in a booth with a view of the boat harbor. We were drinking margaritas the size of wading pools and eating something with a lot of oregano in it. The light poles over the docks swayed in the storm, their hot white mercury lamps reflected in the quivering water of the marina below. I could just make out the hulking black stern of the *Twin Angels* in slip number 45. Way back, when Herb first started talking about taking the money we'd been saving to buy a real house and instead putting it on a boat, he said, "If we owned our own boat, we could have all the things we ever wanted." How could I have known that the only thing Herb wanted was a boat?

I hadn't set foot onboard the *Twin Angels* in years, and I was feeling bad about that for some reason. Or maybe it was having lost yet another game to the Whales. Or maybe I was missing my girls, who weren't speaking to me since Herb told them about my affair with Jimmy. Or maybe it was this freakishly warm end-of-the-world weather. I was starting to think I needed to go home and patch things up with Herb right then, maybe get him to climb into that big new bathtub with me. But then the referee named Marty walked into the Aztec. He sent me his heat-wave smile, and I returned it before I even realized what I was doing. Terri kicked me under the table.

"Act your age," she said through a mouthful of breadstick. "Jesus! You're a married woman."

Yes, I was a married woman, and starting to feel my age too. The left side of my face was still numb where Glenda Brevnik sucker-punched me. If I ended up with a shiner there would be no stopping the small-town rumors that Herb had finally given me what I deserved.

I almost called it a night and headed for home, but then, over Terri's shoulder, I saw the deck lights on the *Twin Angels* flicker on. Apparently Herb had no intention of waiting alone in our empty house all night. In the morning he would already be onboard the boat, ready to sail. I could hardly blame him. When that little house in the woods was empty, it could be a very lonely place.

Marty came up and stood at the end of our booth. He removed his cap—still young enough to play the gentleman. He had a beautiful head of dark brown hair and teeth like a wall of fresh snow. He looked straight at me. "Good game, ladies," he said, but he barely acknowledged the others.

Terri cut me a look. Lauren and Angela were such straight arrows they didn't notice what was going on. They said hi to Marty and went right back to talking about their children's SAT scores and what colleges they'd applied to. I wondered what they would do with all their free time after their kids left home and their houses were empty.

I looked at the lights on the *Twin Angels* once more, twinkling like stars in the falling rain, and then I stood up and threw some bills on the table. "I gotta go."

Terri just shook her head grimly. She was unaware that I knew that it was her—my so-called best friend—who'd told my husband about Jimmy from my yoga class. Like I said, Terri has a way with words. I should have been finished with her for that. But in a town this small, friends are even harder to hang onto than secrets.

I yanked my coat on. Marty helped me with a sleeve. I said to Terri, "I'll see you at yoga." She just rolled her eyes and took a long gulp of her drink.

"I'll walk you to your car," Marty said.

"You be careful, hon," Lauren Jones said. "It's slippery out there."

She got that right.

Marty held the door open, and we walked out into the roar of the Chinook winds and horizontal rain spray. He clutched my elbow as we navigated our way to my car. "This weather," he said. "So warm! It's only February." I slid into my car and rolled down the window. He was saying, "I don't know what's going to happen if it keeps up this way—"

"Marty," I said, "I don't want to go home."

That stopped him. "Really?"

I could see him trying to read my intentions. He wasn't as good at this as I was.

"I could use a drink," I said.

"I have some beer at the house," he offered. "Or we could go—"

"Beer's fine," I said. "I'll follow you." I rolled my window up.

He practically ran across the icy pavement to his truck.

I started my car and turned on the wipers. The night sky was cloud-smothered, moonless, darker than dark. Thank God the Aztec Boat House blocked the view of the harbor so I didn't have to look at the *Twin Angels* again, didn't have to think about Herb settling into his bunk out there on the boat, getting ready to leave like so many times before. But I did.

I was tired suddenly. My shins ached from skating. My hips burned. I felt my injured eye socket swelling.

Marty's truck eased out of the lot and turned left toward the neighborhoods on the hill above the bay. Somewhere up there was his empty house, his empty bed. Ten miles down the road in the other direction, I had an empty bed of my own in a house full of things that I had thought I wanted. I could've gone home and flicked the lights on and off, sat on that nice warm toilet seat, stood under the hot shower until I dissolved. Or I could've gone down to the marina to the *Twin Angels* and tried to convince Herb that what we were going through wasn't climate change but just a spell of uncommon weather.

But I'm one small person, and there are things I can fix and things I really can't.

Do I believe that carrying a canvas bag to the Safeway will help? Riding my bike to work? Sorting my recycling? I'm sorry, but I don't. I've lived most of my adult life without modern conveniences, and yet the polar ice caps are melting and the sea that my husband loves more than me is rising up to swallow the land anyhow.

Do I believe that if I had been a better wife, a better person, Herb would have had more than those three mean words to say to me? That my daughters would speak to me again? Return my calls? Maybe.

But that rainy winter night, I just wanted to be in love once more. Or to *believe* that I was—if just for a little while. I knew that I couldn't make that happen, not with Herb, not with Jimmy from yoga, and not with Marty the referee either. All I could do was put the car in gear and start it rolling forward, the wet beams of my headlights holding all the promise that remained in this big warming world.

Special

Chaz pulled his mother's Outback into the snowed-over lot and parked it under the Alaska Recreational Area sign, gaping through the windshield at the three bodies clad in snow-machine suits lying face down on the surface of the still-frozen lake. Another meth or oxy deal gone sideways? Heroin? Fentanyl maybe. The locals in the jacked-up school buses and Tyvek-covered shacks in the hills above town were as rough as the muffler-bashing roads they lived on. That was true. But still, in the middle of a lake, in the middle of the day? The only other vehicle in the snowy lot was a rusted Toyota stakebed that looked old enough to have come across from Asia on the land bridge.

He reached for his phone just as one of the dead men raised an arm off the ice and then lowered it again as though waving. Chaz stopped. One of the other bodies did the same thing, a dead arm coming up off the ice and going back down again. And then the third body did it too and Chaz understood they were ice fishermen, lying on their bellies, looking into the holes they'd augered there, jigging. He put the phone down.

Jesus. Ice fishing. And he thought *he* was bored.

It was the third week of May and sunny, actual springtime at sea level in the little town on the bay, daffodils thick along the south wall of the Save U More, newborn moose calves tottering through intersections on knobby stilts, piles of dog shit rising like the undead on every thawing lawn. But here, a thousand feet up, aging snow blanketed the ground, and the naked shore alders shuddered miserably in the wind off the still-frozen lake.

He slumped back in his seat, squinting past the prostrate fishermen. Beyond them the dense spruce forests stretched endlessly. Wilderness. God's worst idea ever.

It was Sunday, almost noon, and this was exactly everything he had to do. All day.

It didn't help that Nettle had brought some hipster dickhead home from Humboldt to share her bed in her folks' house and work on the family halibut boat for the summer. Chaz should've seen that coming. At Thanksgiving she'd told him that it was "important to experience all kinds of experiences." In January she'd gone back to California a week before classes restarted. She hadn't come home for spring break at all.

His best friend, Evan, had said, "Chaz, you fag, remember that SAT question: How soon will a girl in college dump her dumbass boyfriend who's still in high school in Fartfuck, Alaska? Surely you picked A. The minute she runs into some rock-star wannabe with a bag of weed in one hand and his dick in the other. Surely, dawg."

This was *exactly* why Chaz was sitting in his mother's car watching guys lolling around on ice like pinnipeds instead of spending the afternoon at Evan's getting high and playing Guitar Hero: Warriors of Rock. *Exactly.*

Ice fishing. Jesus.

He tipped the seat all the way back and closed his eyes.

When he opened his lids again the lake was a barren white pan with three dark holes drilled in it, the parking lot empty as well. The sky was going translucent with streaks of high shredded clouds. The air in the car had cooled. He shivered and sat up. It was nearly time to go home. Time to tell his parents that he was leaving for basic training in two weeks.

The recruiter, a friendly square-jawed guy who looked barely old enough to be out of high school himself, had arrived in town earlier that spring, just a few excruciating weeks after Nettle kicked Chaz's heart out of his chest once and for all. Chaz signed the same day his acceptance to Humboldt arrived—the only college he'd applied to, although he'd led the folks to believe he'd tried for their East Coast alma maters as well.

Well, there was no going to Humboldt now. He didn't need to spend his freshman year spanieling Nettle as she hooked up with one older guy after another. Even *he* knew that.

He shook his head and muttered, "Women."

The week the recruiter was in town, his mother and six other women her age had marched bare-breasted into the high school to protest the military recruiting there. Chaz watched in horror as the topless women argued with the authorities in the school commons, which was crammed with students. His so-called best friend Evan laughed so hard he'd buckled over and cut his head on the door of his locker and had to go to the nurse. Chaz felt queasy himself. There was really no way to prepare yourself for seeing your mother perp-walked out of your school, naked breasts quivering with indignation. Even so, looking back on it, Chaz had to admit that—as responses go—enlisting may have been a little over the top.

*   *   *

In the kitchen that morning he'd come so close to telling his parents what he'd done.

So close. The sun had been shining, and they were cooking together and listening to Neil Young. For old folks it couldn't get much better than that. It would've been a perfect time to say it.

Felix, Marylin, I have something to tell you.

He'd sat at the table nursing his coffee, watching Marilyn wrestle a heavy copper-bottomed pan onto the big five-burner stove.

She glanced his way and said, "Chaz, honey, you can't mope your whole life away over one girl. Take a drive. Take the Subaru. I filled it yesterday."

Chaz grunted noncommittally.

"And don't just go over to Evan's and get high and play video games all day." Marilyn crouched over a low drawer, looking for the pan lid. "Get some sunshine. Vitamin D. It's been a long winter." There was a pause. "Or . . ." Her eyebrows shot up. "You could cook with us!"

She was fucking serious.

How could someone give birth to a person, live with him for eighteen years, and still not know one single thing about him? How was that possible? Cooking with his parents?

Jesus. Really, Jesus.

Felix came out of the walk-in pantry knotting his apron behind him. "Your mother's right, Chazbo. Cooking will get the girl off your mind. It's meditative." He stirred through a drawer of clattering kitchen implements, came up with something made of shiny chrome Chaz hadn't seen before. "Plus, I'm telling you, chicks can't keep their hands off a guy who can handle an herb mincer."

Chaz smiled.

Marilyn laughed. "That's right. Listen to your father, honey. Forget about Nettle. There are lots of other fish, as they say. Next year at college . . ."

Well, that was the whole problem, wasn't it? It was time to tell them that the current dearth of female appendages clutching at him wasn't the only thing on his mind today. He opened his mouth to say it. "I joined the—"

But the folks were on a tear now. Marilyn came up behind Felix and raised a hand to stroke the shiny top of his head. An avalanche of bracelets slid to her elbow. "A bald man in an apron," she said. "Yum."

Neil Young moaned from the speakers.

Chaz studied the bottom of his cup.

For almost a year now, the folks had been enjoying a surge of late-in-life, prescription drug–fueled concupiscence. When their howling had first penetrated his bedroom wall, Chaz asked his sister Ariel to talk to them before she left for college again. "Ariel, seriously!" he pleaded. "It sounds like they're filming a nature special in there."

Ariel had grinned. "Imagine what it *looks* like."

Jesus, he missed his sister.

As always, Ariel was off somewhere doing God knows what between semesters, and Marilyn and Felix were still apparently determined to relive their youths, one orgasm at a time. That was none of his business. Fine. But listening to the gross soundtrack of their exuberant humping was a major downside.

Chaz decided to make a break for it before they started rolling around on the kitchen floor. He grabbed his canvas Carhartt coat. All the senior boys were wearing them that winter. "Goodbye, horny old people," he said, heading for the door.

Marilyn called out after him, "Be home for dinner, sweetie. There's going to be a surprise guest. Have fun!"

Fun? In a town whose sole movie theater was in a Quonset hut? He was eighteen years old. He shouldn't even know what a Quonset hut is. Could there be a worse place than Alaska to be a teenager? He doubted it.

* * *

Driving from the lake back down to town, he decided to tell them over dinner, when spirits were always highest. The surprise guest would be no problem. There *were* no surprise guests. He knew all of Marilyn and Felix's friends. Like his parents, most had arrived there at the end of the road in the '70s: Peace Corps vets, VISTA volunteers, adventure travelers, painters and potters and weavers and musicians and optimistic vegetarian homesteaders. They'd come to Alaska to grow their own groceries, children, and cannabis. By now they'd mostly taken up meat eating, traded their Volkswagen vans for Subarus and Priuses; left their off-the-grid cabins for fully plumbed homes with ocean views, good kitchens, and Wi-Fi. They'd all known each other for decades and, it seemed to Chaz, had all been married or otherwise attached to each other at one time or another as well. The parentage and step-parentage of the children in the town was as complex as a strand of DNA—another reason nobody called anyone Mom or Dad.

Coming up the porch stairs, he decided to blurt it out before the house filled with sub-geezers shouting politics over their salmon carpaccio. But when he opened the back door, there was a red leather suitcase he recognized parked in the entry hall. He sucked in a breath of foody kitchen air and said, "Ariel."

As if conjured by the utterance of her name, his sister stepped into the hallway. Ariel. Home. She'd missed Thanksgiving, Christmas, and spring break, hadn't been spotted in over a year. In fact, she rarely made contact at all—except to arrange for another infusion of cash from the folks.

Were Marilyn and Felix upset about any of that? About anything Ariel did? Ever? No way. Ariel was being independent, colorful. She wasn't missing semesters of college. She was traveling, becoming a citizen of the planet. When she wrote from Amsterdam, "I'm living entirely on hash and sex," the folks swooned in a fond remembrance of debaucheries past. They'd once been smokers of all things smokable, snorters of that which needed snorting, poppers of pills with kicky insider nicknames they still remembered. They'd done it all. Everything. And back when it was still meaningful, they were quick to remind you. And poor Ariel kept trying to live up to their standards.

But now she was here, right in front of him, at last. His fabulous sister Ariel: Evergreen College, class of whatever future year she ran out of majors to switch to or charm enough to talk Felix into bankrolling.

They stood studying each other in the back hallway. Ariel looked older, a little thicker, but even more beautiful than he remembered. She was wearing the lightweight black cashmere sweater he'd sent her for Christmas—the tip of her Sanskrit tattoo showed at her cleavage—tucked into tight black jeans, a silver-studded concho belt. On her feet, blood-red witch boots with black Velcro straps and two-inch heels.

She was bald.

That was new. What had happened to the massive basket of red-blond dreads she'd first cultivated in ninth grade? A look that Marilyn had attempted to match in misguided solidarity until Ariel promised to murder her mother in her sleep if she saw a single small cornrow anywhere near that middle-aged scalp.

Ariel, bald now?

Chaz stood there grinning. Not even Marilyn would try to expropriate this stunt.

Ariel reached over and yanked the canvas collar of his coat straight. "Carhartt?" She grimaced. "Eee-eye, eee-eye, oh." She pushed past him, a whiff of citrus lingering in the air behind her. "Duck hunting now, Chazzy?"

"I sort of went ice fishing today," he said, and found himself so happy he started to cry.

Into the pantry closet she went, as if her appearance there was entirely normal, as if it hadn't been months since she'd finally answered her only brother's pathetic messages about Nettle's betrayal—Ariel's voice on the phone from God knows where, booming drunkenly, "Forget that little twat, Chaz. And don't do anything stupid! You hear me? In this family *I'm* in charge of stupid!"

Too late.

If Ariel had been there, she would have shoved those papers up that friendly recruiter's friendly ass.

Now Chaz watched her disappear into the pantry, the top of her skull mossed with blond fuzz. He sniffed and wiped his eyes.

Note to self: no crying in boot camp.

Ariel. Still trying to outdo the folks. She'd been working at it a long time. The dungeon vampire slut phase. The blessedly brief vegan era (which Marilyn, to her credit, stoically cooked right through as though she actually considered lentils edible). The excruciating "men in uniform" phase (which, to Felix's obvious relief, had been another short one, but only because there was just a small Coast Guard contingent on the bay and not a naval base). Chaz had watched in amazement as Marilyn and Felix proclaimed each nightmare Ariel unleashed on them artistic, inventive, original. Because, above and beyond all else, in a town crawling with more-interesting-than-average children, it was important that theirs were special.

"You're the surprise guest?" Chaz said, as Ariel rummaged in the pantry. "I was hoping it would be an old nun maybe, or the produce guy from Safeway. Someone, you know, interesting."

She laughed, but he still felt his mood sag, suddenly wondering why she was home now. Yes, it was the end of the semester, but wasn't there some Reid College, beret-wearing jerkwad out there waiting for her in an organic opium den somewhere? This little town—eight bars and a community college, nine churches and who knows how many charter boats—clinging to the tail end of the continent like the last flea on very large dog, couldn't possibly be the most interesting place Ariel could find to spend the summer. That would be too horrible. Something was up.

Ariel came out of the pantry hefting a dark wine bottle. She appraised him with older sister impunity, tossing the bottle from palm to palm. "Ice fishing in a farmer coat, Chaz? God, that little bitch really creamed you."

Chaz began to say that he was over Nettle, but a sudden calamitous crashing of pots and pans rang out in the kitchen.

Ariel jumped, barely catching the wine bottle against the sweater Chaz had paid a fortune for. On Christmas Eve he'd given an identical one to Nettle, and she'd declared it "bourgeois" and laid it back in its tissue-lined box saying she was concerned that they didn't share the same "moral core," that they didn't "value the same values." Apparently, she'd been right.

But loyal Ariel was wearing her sweater, and now she clutched the bottle even tighter against it with mock horror. "I drop this baby, Felix rewrites the will."

And then all the sarcastic silliness left her face. She bit her lip and sighed. "Christ, Chaz. You look like shit. The next time I see Nettle I'm going to gouge her fucking eyes out."

Chaz threw his arms around her and crushed her to him. "How long will you be here?" He pressed his cheek against her ear and squeezed until the wine bottle dug into his breastbone. "How long?"

"I'm going to drop it!" she screamed, laughing.

"Oh, lunatics," Marilyn sang from the kitchen, "that's a very good pinot!"

"Ariel!" Chaz hugged her even harder. "How long do you have?"

*　*　*

Over dinner—Marilyn and Felix's specialty: local sablefish in a vodka/tomato cream sauce, lemon risotto, green beans with fresh mozzarella—Ariel regaled them with tales of her travels with the boyfriend *du jour*. Marilyn and Felix reminisced about countries they'd hitchhiked across in the '70s. Felix seemed pleased to hear that Turkey was just as Turkish as it had been when he last checked. Marilyn tried to steer the conversation around to Morocco, but Ariel wanted to talk about Tunisia instead. Or something. Chaz was not following closely. He ate silently, watching his wild and beautiful sister working hard at being her wild and beautiful self, and waiting for an opportunity to tell everyone what he'd done.

His mother had shifted gears—and continents. "After Bali, I hitched a boat ride to Darwin. In those days, Northern Australia was so—" Marilyn stopped midsentence. She looked at Chaz and then at Ariel. "This conversation is boring your brother, dear. Maybe if he had something more interesting to offer?" She gave Chaz a withering look.

"Me?" Chaz scoffed. "You guys are boring and that's *my* fault somehow?"

Ariel raised her eyebrows appreciatively. "Touché."

Marilyn frowned, stirring a string bean through the sheen of cream sauce on her plate. She looked across the table at Felix as if she thought he, husband and father, should do or say something about this.

"What?" Felix said, and unconsciously left his mouth hanging open.

There was a small pink crescent of sauce on his chin. In the dense silence, Ariel reached over and dabbed at it with her napkin, gently pushing her father's jaw shut in the process. Then Marilyn snorted, and the whole table exploded into laughter.

"Me, boring?" Felix roared, hammering the table. "I'll drink to that!"

Marilyn shrieked, hurled a gulp of wine down her throat, and shrieked again. Ariel guffawed, clutching her stomach. They couldn't get it under control. They didn't want to. This was what they loved most. Barely contained chaos. They laughed at the din of their own laughter—Marilyn baying like a coyote, Ariel squealing with hilarity, Felix choking and coughing and laughing and laughing and laughing.

"Boring?" Felix gasped, and they laughed harder still.

Chaz tried to laugh too, but without much success, given that he could end the hilarity with four simple words. Once again he made the decision to tell them. But even as he did, he noticed the tears coursing down his sister's cheeks.

They weren't the tears of gaiety wetting Marilyn's face, or Felix's. These were running from the laughter, not with it. And then it hit him. Ariel was sick. She hadn't shaved her head to get even more attention. She was bald because she was sick! That's why she'd come home. She'd tried to keep it from Marilyn and Felix as long as she could. But now she'd come back to them, as though they could somehow get her out of this trouble—like everything else they'd fixed for her. Why else would she take time out from her travels, her adventures, her love affairs?

Why? Because she was really, really sick.

Chaz waited, something tugging at a nerve in the right side of his neck.

They finally pulled themselves together, sipped their wine, dabbed the corners of their eyes. Felix sighed, "Oh, brother," and speared the last lambent sliver of fish on his plate. Ariel held her arms tight across her sweater and let out a long whoosh of air.

Chaz watched his sister carefully, the idea of her sickness growing inside him like . . . well, like a sickness. Some metaphors can't be improved upon. She seemed smaller now, softer, and fragile too. Ariel, fragile? That was a word he would never have imagined in the same breath as her name.

Their parents still couldn't see it, Chaz realized. They refused to figure it out for themselves, and Ariel was not intending to tell them until it was impossible to hide. He knew her that well, even if they didn't. She was sick and she was embarrassed by that and had been covering it up, trying to make the shaved head look like a statement of some kind. But sooner or later it had to come out, because there was no way to be sick ironically, no way to make being sick cool or smart. Sickness was not special. It was common. Anybody could get sick. Ariel wasn't going to admit to being that ordinary until she absolutely had to. And neither were Marilyn and Felix.

Felix smiled fondly at Ariel. "I gotta tell you, I love that dome. You look more like me than ever."

Ariel leaned almost out of her chair, grinning. She put one hand behind Felix's neck, pulling her father to her. They touched the tops of their hairless heads together.

"Let me get a picture!" Marilyn leapt out of her seat.

Felix and Ariel remained leaning into each other as if joined at the skull.

Marilyn was already back, snapping the photo on her phone.

Before he could stop himself, Chaz said, "Ariel, are you going to tell them about the hairdo?"

Ariel pulled away from her father and straightened in her chair. "Sure," she said calmly. But she gave him a look that he couldn't read. Was she bluffing? Or not? "Sure," she said again, more cheerily.

Marilyn still clutched the phone in both hands. "What?" Her eyes glistened with anticipation. "Is it a surprise? Wait! Let me get dessert."

"Ariel just wants to look like me," Felix said, gently patting the top of his head. "Lots of women do. It's a thing."

Ariel stared across the table at Chaz a moment longer. Something in her eyes dimmed and then relit itself as if she had taken a deep breath, though she hadn't. Then, with the magnetic charm once more radiating from her like a birthing star, she blithely launched into a story about her friends at school all shaving their heads in support of women in the shoe factories of Bosnia. Or maybe it was Botswana. Chaz tuned it out.

Marilyn and Felix were listening, though, and that was the important thing. They were enthralled again, devouring what Ariel was saying, pleased that she, their daughter, was carrying on the work that they had started so long ago, the hard, hard work of being interesting.

"I have a surprise too," Chaz whispered. But nobody seemed to hear him.

* * *

At the lake, after the ice fishermen had gone, he'd walked down to the shore through the aging granulated snow, the wind like a hand between his shoulder blades urging him out onto the ice. A gust slammed across the lake and sent a long shiver through the tops of the spruce forest on the far shore. He zipped the heavy canvas coat up and knelt at one of the holes the men had left, and then lay with his chin on the small mound of ice chips surrounding the hole, his hands shading his face like horse blinders as he peered into the clear water. Halfway down, perhaps six feet below him, a Dolly Varden char hovered, suspended in the water column, motionless but for the smallest movements of its white-rimmed pectoral fins. Its lavender torpedo form was dotted with dreamy pink spots, the tip of its snout a flaming yellow-orange. Even by trout standards, the fish was extreme, extravagant, extraordinary.

Chaz whispered to it, "I joined the army."

* * *

They were raving about the dessert now.

Not sure what Marilyn had put in front of him, Chaz lifted a spoonful to his lips. The food acknowledged, his sister went back to her story, and his parents joined in from time to time, Felix saying, "I read something about those factories somewhere," Marilyn groaning with weary indignation, "It never ends."

Chaz let the sugary dessert melt on his tongue as Ariel, his beautiful bald sister, rambled on, clearly knowing, as Chaz knew, that their parents, Marilyn and Felix, would not only believe her but were already forming the idea of retelling this story themselves, at this very table, over some of the best damn meals you could find at the end of a road to nowhere, savoring the idea of sharing it with their friends, again and again and again, for years to come—even long after their children were gone.

Acknowledgments

I would like to thank the editors and staff of the publications where these stories first appeared.

Alaska Quarterly Review: "Every Son Must Wonder"
   (as "Halfway")
Anchorage Press: "Little Wing" (as "Twirlers")
Bull: "Time on the Water"
Catamaran Literary Review: "Help" and "Xtratuf"
Fiction Southeast: "Chekhov's Rule"
Gray's Sporting Journal: "Mammoth"
Permafrost: "So, Kenny the Sheetrocker Sends for His Girl"
South Dakota Review: "Special" and "Angels, Jellies, and Squid"
The Sun: "Uncommon Weather"

I would also like to thank the many good friends and colleagues who read, encouraged, and/or advised on these stories and others over the years—with apologies to those I'm surely forgetting: Ed Allen, Jim Babb, Scott Banks, Susan Banks, Jay Bechtol, Bob Bundy, Anne Coray, Ann Dixon, Nick Dighiera, Mike Floyd, Justin Herrmann, Mary Katzke, Ann Kefer, Tom Kizzia, Mary Langham, Nancy Lord, Jo-Ann Mapson, Valerie Miner, Linda Martin, Lou Martinez, Ed Murphy, Bradford Philen, Bill Rice, Zack Rogow, Teresa Sundmark, Sarah Swandel, Geffery Von Gerlach, Miranda Weiss, and Dave Zoby. Thanks to the Alaska State Council on the Arts for their generous support.

And, as always, my number one reader, Lin Hampson.